"I got him for you, Kelsey!" the ambusher boasted. "Now we can have their gold."

Billy watched the dying Kelsey and his partner a moment, then swung a Winchester toward them.

"Hold there!" Billy called. "Drop your rifle!"

Quick as a flash the rifleman turned and tried to fire. But before the Sharps could send its deadly load Billy's way, the Winchester fired.

All Billy could think as he watched the assassin fall was that the killing had returned, just as it always had....

PURGATORY

G. Clifton Wisler

FAWCETT GOLD MEDAL • NEW YORK

for my sister Karen

CHAPTER 1

It was a pale, grayish, late-autumn kind of morning. A haze clung to the yellowing prairies of southwestern Colorado and shrouded the distant Spanish Peaks. Years before, great herds of buffalo would have been making their way across the grasslands, growing their winter coats even as Arapaho and Cheyenne hunting parties stalked their trail.

Seven hard winters had visited the plains since the territorial cavalry had ridden down Black Kettle's camp at Sand Creek, staining the rocky ground with the blood of innocents and breaking the old chief's heart. Even now the wind seemed to carry the cries of dying women and children as it howled across the land. Four years later Custer had finished the southern Cheyenne at the Washita River. The pitiful survivors had been rounded up and carried away. The great pony herd had been massacred with its owners.

The Indians were gone. White men had yet to carve up the open range. The territorial capital at Denver thrived. Veterans of the cruel Civil War flocked there, lured by gold strikes and tales of riches beyond belief. Since the great rush of '59, a huddle of mining communities had appeared to the north and west of the capital, living and dying as the streams gave forth their treasure.

Here, farther south, a seemingly endless prairie stretched on toward Texas. The fledgling town of Trinidad had sprung up where the road to Santa Fe crossed the Purgatory River. Few other signs of permanent settlement could be detected. Statehood remained a distant hope, and the country was left to fend for itself.

More than anything, it was a place for wayfarers. Gypsy miners roamed the mountain streams, gambling their lives that gold enough for a lifetime lay just over the next hill. Cardsharps and outlaws who preyed on the isolated miners and the freight traffic moving between Denver and Santa Fe abounded. There were, too, old frontiersmen who abandoned the wild days of their youth and fought to reconcile themselves with the encroaching fingers of civilization. Mexican families, displaced by the growing Anglo presence in the New Mexico Territory, sought a new life in the shadow of the high mountains.

Above all else, Colorado held out the promise of hope, of fresh beginnings. Men who'd worn the blue or the gray set aside their swords and tried to forget. Families who'd watched their homes being devoured by flames or stolen away by carpetbagging politicians sought out land where they could build anew.

It was that promise of starting fresh that brought a solitary rider southward from Pueblo through the amber grass, past the bones of slaughtered buffalo and the charred remains of Cheyenne campgrounds. Under the worn brim of a Confederate cavalry officer's hat, two sad eyes scanned the horizon, seeking out a refuge from the living death he'd known since leaving his home ten long years before.

"Always it comes back," he mumbled as he recalled the terrifying charges across hillsides from Shiloh to the Wilderness. And there was the recent madness, the lifeless bodies he'd left behind in the streets of Cimarron, the smoke of black powder that still stung his eyes, the smell and taste of death that clung to a man, that resisted all manner of cleansing.

He looked toward the narrow channel of the Purgatory River as it churned through the prairie, bound for eventual union with the mighty Arkansas up north. He scratched his bearded cheeks and stared at the clouds over the mountains to the west. Once before he'd ridden into the Rockies. It was the Bighorn country that time, back in '67 when he'd abandoned the hope of returning to Texas, of finding the dream of his youth, of riding the Brazos as his father had promised.

Yes, the dream was dead, shot down at Shiloh with the man who'd helped to shape it. Now everything was confused, clouded by a hundred memories that could not, would not be forgotten. Each time it seemed he'd touch some particle of gentleness, discover some moment of peace, the killing always came back to drive him away.

"Purgatory," he said, drawing his spotted mustang pony to a halt. The name seemed appropriate. His whole world since Appomattox had drifted alternately through heaven and hell as if fate couldn't seem to make up its mind what to do with him.

He scratched his beard again. He was dusty, weary from days and weeks of drifting that had grown into months. Soon it would be winter. Where would it find him this year? Stumbling around the saloons and hotel parlors of Wichita or Abilene, walking the streets of some ramshackle town, preparing to meet the challenge of some faceless man who also wore a long-barreled Colt on his hip? Perhaps this time it wouldn't be the faceless stranger whose broken body lay in the dust, the life flowing out of him.

"No!" he shouted across the emptiness. "No!"

He nudged the pony on toward the river. There had to be something better. He'd put the past behind him, hadn't he? The old trunk with its trophies of battle, its reminders of the old dream, of the boy he'd been—all that was safely stored away in a freight warehouse in Pueblo. He'd even

3

given up the proud black stallion and the spry mare he'd ridden along the Cimarron months before when he'd been Billy Starr. That name—Starr—had sent children trembling to their beds on stormy nights.

Yes, he'd put it all aside: the clothes, the horses, the reputation. If only he could erase the memories as easily. If only he could forget the eyes of all those men, the dying and the maimed. It was their curse, and it would plague him to his grave. He understood that much.

When he reached the bank of the river, he slid down from his saddle and dipped his hand into the shallow water. Already there was a hint of winter in the stream. Winter should be a time to rest. It should be passed in the warmth of a house, shared with those who loved and were loved. There should be time to pause and to plan the next crop, to contemplate another long cattle drive up the trail from Palo Pinto to Abilene. But there were no soft shoulders to lie beside in the cold of a December night, no laughing voices to chase through the house, no tenderness at all.

He closed his eyes for a moment and fought to recall another time, another river. But it had all been too long ago, and he had been another man. He blinked away the sadness and filled his hands with water. As the liquid touched his parched lips, he thought back to the other times he'd tried to start anew, in the Bighorn country in the north and in the fledgling cattle towns of Kansas. Each time he'd tried to build a new life, clouds from the past had returned. Well, maybe the shadows would fade with the passage of time. Perhaps he would find release from his ghosts in Trinidad.

He hoped so.

What will it be this time? he asked himself. The name. Willie Delamer had been abandoned long ago, left behind like the trunk, awaiting the day when he might be able to go back.

"I can't use Starr," he mumbled. Nor Fletcher, either. He'd given that name at the livery in Pueblo. It must be

4

something simple, a name that wouldn't attract notice. Cook? Yes, that was it; Billy Cook.

Sure, that sounded innocent enough. No one would imagine Billy Cook capable of meting out death as a Mississippi riverboat gambler dealt cards. Sure. Billy Cook would do.

CHAPTER 2

Trinidad was a typical southwestern town. There were two parallel lines of adobe dwellings at the southern end of a single street. At the north end of town stood a single two-story structure, flanked by two smaller buildings made of pine pickets. Over the porch of the larger place was a sign reading Trinidad Hotel.

The man who now called himself Billy Cook urged his horse into a slow trot and continued down the street. He drew in the reins as he reached the hotel. There was a lone hitching post beside the porch, and he dismounted, then tied the mustang's lead securely to the post.

"Rest easy, boy," Billy said, patting the animal's nose. "I'll find you some hay."

The horse dipped its head, and Billy turned toward the hotel. He stepped inside the lobby and made his way to the front desk. After a few minutes, he located the clerk.

"I need a room," Billy informed the man.

"Well, mister, that's your trouble," the clerk said, turning back to some papers.

"I'm a paying customer, not some vagabond lost on his way to Denver."

"Mister, I couldn't care if you were Ulysses Simpson Grant. This hotel's got seven rooms, and there's not a one of 'em's not rented."

"Any other hotel in town?" Billy asked.

"Nope," the clerk answered, shaking his head.

"Rooming house?"

"Not a one."

"So what does a visitor do for a roof over his head in this town?"

"Well, I suppose he persuades somebody to shorten his stay at the hotel. Or else he marries one of the Martinez girls."

The clerk laughed, but Billy wasn't amused. He turned away from the desk and marched out of the hotel. He untied his horse and led it along until he spotted a sign outside one of the adobe huts.

"Silverado Saloon," Billy mumbled. A less appropriate name for the place wasn't possible. Still, it'd been days since he'd had anything but dried beef and beans to eat, much less a taste of spirits. He tied the mustang to one of the porch posts and walked inside.

The interior of the saloon was filled with smoke. Through it Billy detected a trio of men gambling at a round table near the door. Two teamsters sat on stools by the bar.

"Can I get you something?" the bartender asked.

"Cold beer," Billy said, climbing onto a bar stool.

"Got some beer, but it's none too cold," the bartender said.

"Will be come winter," one of the teamsters said. The others laughed.

"I've got a bit of St. Louis whiskey," the bartender whispered to Billy. "It's four bits a shot. The other stuff's local, but it's half the price."

Billy placed a quarter on the bar, and the bartender filled a small glass from a dark-colored bottle. Billy sipped

7

the liquor, feeling his throat catch fire as the alcohol burned its way through his system.

"Another?" the bartender asked.

"No. That'll do," Billy said.

The bartender shrugged his shoulders and turned back to the teamsters. Billy climbed off his stool and joined the gamblers.

"Care to take a hand?" asked a tall man dressed in dark leather.

"Might," Billy said. "If it's not a private affair."

"No, we need some fresh blood." The second man spoke up. His accent was eastern, and he wore a satin vest over a lace shirt. The third man, another teamster by the look of his dusty clothes and rough hands, raked in the cards and dealt four new hands.

"They call me Stephens," the first man said, examining Billy through suspicious eyes. "Hart Stephens. Maybe you heard of me?"

"No," Billy said. "Should I have?"

"Oh, there are those who'd say I was a man to know hereabouts," Stephens said, smiling.

"Hart here's the one who shot old Santa Cruz Simpson dead as a doornail last July," the teamster said.

"I haven't heard of Simpson, either," Billy said, discarding two useless cards and keeping three assorted spades as the bets were placed. "But then I haven't been down in this part of the territory much."

"Where have you been?" Stephens asked.

"Here and there," Billy said. "Here and there."

Neither of the two replacement cards were spades, but there was a second seven and an even more valuable second queen. Stephens appeared quite disturbed when Billy's two pair won the hand.

"Lady Luck smiles early on the stranger," the easterner declared. "They call me Ernest Brown, out of Cincinnati. Don't believe I caught your name."

"Probably didn't," Billy said.

Stephens refilled his glass from a tall bottle of rye whiskey, then did likewise for Brown and the teamster. Billy frowned. He never enjoyed the prospect of walking into a setup game.

"Hey, boy, how 'bout bringin' us another bottle?" Stephens called out, banging his hand on the table. "A little service, sonny!"

Billy noticed for the first time a slightly built young man wearing a white apron. Shaggy blond hair fell down toward the boy's eyes, and it wasn't until he drew near that Billy recognized the youthful face.

"Billy?" the boy said, setting down the bottle and taking a five-dollar bill from Stephens.

"Yes, that's right," Billy said quickly. "Billy . . . Cook."

"You two know each other from before, huh?" Stephens asked. "Where might that've been?"

"Down in the Cimarron country," the boy explained.

"I did some ranch work for Jason here's pa," Billy said, staring coldly at Stephens.

"They had themselves a top-notch range war goin' up that way last I heard," Stephens said, scratching his left ear. "I heard Luke Hall got himself shot there. Texas Bob Smith, too."

"That's why I left," Billy said. "What's a regular old Texas cowboy supposed to do when people start shooting each other dead? Best to leave while you can, right, Jason?"

"Sure," Jason agreed, turning to go.

"Hold on there, sonny," Stephens said, grabbing the apron and holding the young man in place. "Your old man has a ranch, does he? What'd you be doin' a job like this for?"

"Beats stable work," Jason said, freeing himself.

Stephens started to grab the boy's arm, but a stare from Billy froze his movements.

"Let's play cards," Billy said, taking his turn as dealer.

The game continued, but Stephens's eyes continued to roam around the saloon. Most often they rested on young Jason McNally.

Billy's glance fell there, too. He hasn't changed much, Billy thought, remembering when Jason had left the ranch

9

on that darkest of nights after his father had ordered a dozen farmers and their families shot. The boy had grown a hair, but his eyes were still bright and alive. He was a little thinner, perhaps.

"Three kings," Brown announced when Billy called the hand.

Billy frowned. Among his own cards were the king of hearts and the king of clubs.

"Your deal," Billy said, placing his cards flat on the surface of the table as Brown gathered in his winnings. "In most places, you take all cards off the top of the deck, too, Brown."

"Meaning?" Brown asked.

"I have good eyes," Billy said, leaning back in his chair. "And I prefer the odds in a straight game."

"You sayin' this is somethin' else?" Stephens asked, half rising from his chair.

"Could be," Billy said. "Might just be a mistake. Anybody's entitled to one mistake, isn't he, Mr. Brown?"

Brown's hands trembled slightly as he dealt. Stephens refilled the glasses from the fresh bottle and the whiskey calmed Brown's nerves. All cards were dealt from the top, and there was no reappearance of the mysterious fifth king. Billy played cautiously nevertheless, keeping the wagers small and taking few risks. As a result, most of the money simply moved around the table, never settling in anyone's hands for long. Billy himself accumulated a little more than fifty dollars before they stopped to eat lunch.

"We can eat and play at the same time," Brown said as Billy rose from the table.

"You can," Billy said, walking to the bar. "I never mix the business of eating with the pleasure of gambling."

Stephens laughed, but Brown continued to look nervous. Billy ignored them both and sat down at the bar.

"Another glass now, mister?" the bartender asked.

"Something to eat," Billy told him. "You can find me some food, can't you?"

"Cantina down the street's got tamales, beans."

"I've had a gullet full of beans. Tamales will do if there's nothing else to be had."

"Jason, boy, fetch some tamales for this man!" the bartender hollered.

"I'll see what I can find you, Billy," Jason whispered as he passed Billy on the way to the door. "I know the cook."

A few minutes later Jason returned carrying a platter of hot tamales covered with chili. In addition there were a half-dozen slices of beef, some potatoes, and even two carrots.

"You're a wonder, Jason McNally," Billy said, following the young man to an empty table. "Carrots? Where did you locate them?"

"Maria gets tired of tamales and beans, too. I talked her out of this, but it'll cost you two dollars instead of six bits."

"Fair bargain, Jason. Keep one for yourself, too," Billy added, handing over three large government notes. "Tell me. What do you know about the three cardplayers?"

"Stephens has been here since spring. Loman was working for Art Clancy's freight company."

"Was?"

"Got sent packing. He was caught with his hand in the till."

"And Brown?"

"Got in last week. Watch him, Billy. He'd steal your drawers in a bathhouse. He cheats at cards."

"I noticed."

"And you didn't call him?"

"What would that've proved? Somebody would've died."

"I've seen Stephens," Jason said, laughing. "He's not so much. You could take him."

"Is that why you left your father's ranch, to watch more men die?" Billy asked.

"No." Jason sighed.

"Me, neither. I'm tired of the killing."

"You won't call a man for cheatin', so you won't make

11

much of a gambler. You're through hirin' out your gun. So what're you going to do?"

"Who knows? Maybe I'll go back to the Comanche. I lived with them before. And what about yourself? This isn't exactly a step up for you, Jason."

"A man's got to eat."

"That he does," Billy said, slapping the young man on the shoulder. "Now, are you going to let me eat all this myself?"

Jason smiled and grabbed a tamale. Before long the two of them had emptied the platter.

"You comin' back to the table, Cook?" Stephens called out when Billy got to his feet.

"I think maybe you three ought to go on ahead," Billy said. "I really don't have my mind on the game now."

"Too busy talkin' over old times with sonny there?" Stephens asked. "Hey, boy, when are you gettin' around to fetchin' us some dinner?"

The bartender motioned for Jason to go to the card table. Jason approached it cautiously.

"That sure is a nice apron you got yourself there," Loman said, tearing the piece of cloth from Jason's waist. "Got yourself done up like a regular little Miss Cook. Cook. Ain't that your name, stranger? Maybe you two are related. This belong to you, huh, mister?"

The teamster waved the apron at Billy. The bartender started to intervene, but Stephens waved him back to the bar. The other saloon customers slipped outside.

"How 'bout it, Cook?" Loman asked. "This belong to you?"

Billy's face began to redden. He started toward Loman, but Jason dashed in front, snatched the apron, and stepped back as Loman swung a heavy hand out. The blow narrowly missed. A second landed, though, sending Jason flying across the floor of the saloon. Loman followed, laughing as he drove the toe of his boot into young Jason's ribs.

"That's about enough!" Billy cried, picking up a chair

12

and slamming it across Loman's forehead. The big teamster groaned as he fell.

"Look out!" Jason yelled as Stephens reached for his pistol. Billy slung a second chair at the gunman, then ducked as Brown slammed a bottle against the table, just missing him. A quick left sent Loman reeling. Brown then raced out the open doors into the street.

"Looks like it's just the two of us now," Billy said, squaring off against Stephens. "You really want to continue this discussion?"

"Oh, we're a long ways from finished with this," Stephens said, gazing at the floor where his pistol lay.

"It's not in my mind to kill anyone today," Billy said, fingering his own Colt. "But if I have to . . ."

"You'll be dying soon enough, Cook," Stephens called out. "You, too, sonny."

Jason turned a bit pale, but Billy drew his pistol in a flash and blasted the deserted poker table. Cards flew into the air, and Stephens instinctively ducked.

"I could've just as easily put you in your grave just then," Billy said. "And I'll do it yet if I hear any threats toward me or young Jason. Now get out!"

Stephens stumbled over to his gun, but Billy kicked it across the room.

"You won't need that. Go!" Billy said.

Stephens staggered over to where Loman lay. The two of them managed to get outside.

"Mister, you'd best make a quick retreat," the bartender said.

"Here's ten dollars for the mess," Billy said. "There's nothing holding me here. I won't dally."

"Billy," Jason said, wiping a trace of blood from his lip. "Billy, you'd best watch your back. Those three won't be forgettin' this."

"Well, neither will I," Billy said, angrily pounding a table. "A man can only be pushed so far."

"Keep an eye out for them."

"I will."

"If you don't get yourself back-shot, maybe we'll cross paths again one of these days," Jason went on.

"Can't ever tell," Billy said, smiling as he turned toward the door.

Once outside, Billy located Stephens, Loman, and Brown on the porch of the hotel. He untied his horse, then mounted. As he rode out of town, he kept his eyes on the three men he'd so easily converted into enemies.

I never could tolerate towns, Billy thought. No, the only place he was ever really comfortable was out in the countryside, sleeping beneath the stars, feeling one with the world.

It was a lie. He enjoyed a soft bed and a warm fire as much as anyone. It was people he couldn't get used to, especially townspeople. No, he wouldn't miss the people.

CHAPTER 3

Billy should have grown accustomed to leaving. It seemed sometimes he'd spent a lifetime departing one place and setting out for another. So many of his days had been passed wandering aimlessly across the land, searching for some kind of permanence, some refuge from the burdens of his past.

He rode the weary mustang westward along the Purgatory, slowly but surely making his way into the foothills of the Rockies. The distant peaks seemed to hold out promise, hope for something better. But the horse was tired, and Billy reluctantly drew to a halt near a small spring a little less than two miles from town.

"Tomorrow it's back to the high country, boy," Billy said as he dismounted. "There's good grass here and cool water at the spring. It'll make a fine camp."

As Billy loosened the cinch and removed the saddle, he thought of how there should have been someone other than a plains pony to listen to his words. After years of solitary life, he should have adjusted to the terrible silence. But perhaps that wasn't possible.

15

He busied himself that next hour making camp. He spread out his blankets beside a small cook fire. As the sun dipped below the distant mountain slopes, he had a small tin of beans bubbling and some dried beef mixed with onions cooking in a skillet. Telltale traces of chimney smoke from Trinidad curled up from the east.

The crackling of the fire muted the sound of footsteps on the hillside above. Billy never heard the click of the hammers. The pop of a Sharps carbine was the first signal of danger. The shot hit the ground no more than a foot away from Billy's hand. Another scattered twigs in the woodpile. He never heard the third shot, only felt something slam into his right thigh.

He had no time to think, to react. Before he could reach his pistol, two more slugs tore into him, one striking his shoulder, the other hitting him in the chest. His eyes grew watery, and he slumped to the ground.

"Got him!" a voice called out from the aspens on the nearby hillside.

"Stay back, Brown," Hart Stephens warned. "His type can be tricky."

"Tricky, hell," Loman said, stepping boldly from his hiding place. "He's shot to pieces. I never seen a man walk away from three shots like that."

Loman continued toward the fire. When he reached Billy, the teamster turned the wounded man's body onto its side, then laughed.

"I never had myself a pair of boots as good as these," Loman said, prying the boots from Billy's feet.

"I don't suppose he's got much use for 'em," Brown said. "Nor this hat, either. I always wondered what I'd look like as a Reb."

Stephens joined in the laughter. For his part, he seemed uninterested in Billy's clothes. He concentrated instead on going through the pockets of Billy's coat, drawing out the greenbacks and shaking the traces of blood from their corners.

"We agreed, Stephens," Loman said. "Fair split."

"You're takin' his boots," Stephens said. "Brown's got the hat."

"I'll take his coat, also," Loman said, pulling the bloodstained cowhide jacket from Billy's shoulders. "The pistol, too."

"I'll take that from your share," Stephens said. "Here, that leaves you each about eighty."

"Eighty?" Brown asked. "I thought there was nearly four hundred dollars in that stash."

"You want another accountin'?" Stephens asked, tapping the side of his holster.

"No, whatever you say's fair, Hart," Loman said nervously. "No point in squabblin' over such a thing."

"Besides," Stephens said, approaching the spotted pony Billy had left grazing beside the spring, "if you'd handled the cards right, there'd been no need of comin' all the way up here."

"How was I to know he had such a sharp eye, Hart?" Brown complained. "Besides, we'll be back at the hotel without losin' any sleep."

"That's true enough," Stephens said, laughing.

Billy heard it all. The pain swelled up inside him, and he wanted to scream, to clutch something, to strike out with a last dying gasp at his attackers. But there was no power in his fingers and his mind was cloudy. He felt the life flowing out of his chest. Inside he trembled, but he fought back a moan.

"How 'bout I finish him, Hart?" Loman asked, pointing Billy's own revolver at the apparently lifeless man.

"No, let him suffer awhile," Stephens said. "There are wolves hereabouts. Let them have some fun, too. Now help me gather in this pony. We can get a few dollars for him back in town."

But even with the three of them encircling the horse, it would not be trapped. Instead it dashed down the slope and galloped off to the safety of the riverbed.

"Well, you call yourself a teamster!" Stephens yelled at Loman. "Can't even lasso a mustang pony."

"He's likely three-quarters wild," Loman said.

"Wouldn't've brought us anything but grief. People would remember that cowboy rode him out of town. Especially that saloon boy. Marshal might've had some questions."

"I never found questions much of a hindrance," Stephens said. "As for that boy, I've got a score to settle there. I wouldn't let him trouble you much."

The three men laughed again. Then they returned to the rocky hillside above Billy's camp, collected their horses, and headed back toward Trinidad.

Billy wasn't sure what kept him alive that next hour. Maybe it was some inner fury that restored life to his fingers, that cleared his mind long enough to allow him to stuff part of a kerchief into the hole in his thigh and slow the bleeding. The other wounds, though they looked to all eternity to be fatal, were less serious. The bullet that had struck his chest proved to be a spent ball, and the other had passed cleanly through the fleshy part of his shoulder.

Using his elbows, Billy managed to drag himself to the spring. The cool water soothed the aches within his body, and the chill of the evening air slowed the bleeding. But even as he began to allow himself some hope for survival, he heard footsteps nearby.

So, he thought, they've come to finish it after all. He groped for the pistol that was absent from its holster. He reached for the knife in its scabbard on his leg. It, too, was gone, taken along with his boots. In desperation he grasped a nearby rock, but his fingers lacked the strength to raise it from the ground.

So, after so many miles, so many battles, this is it, he thought. He swallowed his pain and stared out past the pale shadow of light that glowed from the coals of his fire.

"Billy?" a voice called out. "Billy, you there?"

"Here." Billy moaned, trying without success to raise himself.

"God, they've killed you," said young Jason McNally, gasping, as he ran to Billy's side. "You've been shot good."

"Worse'n last time, huh?" Billy asked, fighting to keep a faint smile on his face.

"I found your horse," Jason said, pointing back toward the camp. "I followed Stephens and the others out from town. But they headed into the rocks, and I lost 'em. Then I saw the mustang. I knew somethin' was wrong."

"I know better," Billy mumbled as his eyes closed. "You can't let a man have a second shot at you."

"Rest easy. I'll tend to you."

"They'll come for you next, boy," Billy said, clutching Jason's arm. "Have to hide."

"No more hidin'," Jason said. "No more runnin' away. If they come back, they'll be the ones who get the surprise this time."

"Jason . . ."

"Now you leave me to do what's got to be done this time. I've dressed wounds before. I know what to do."

"Be sure to . . . to . . ."

"I know what to do," Jason repeated, tearing fabric to make bandages. "Rest easy."

Billy had little choice. His entire body throbbed with pain, and a great numbness possessed his arms and legs. He grew light-headed, then lapsed into unconsciousness.

CHAPTER 4

When he awoke, Billy found himself lying beneath a makeshift shelter in the rocks above the river. Below, near the spring, the spotted pony grazed beside a roan mare. Billy had lost track of time; he had no notion as to whether he'd slept a day, a week, or a month. But as his head began to clear, he discovered someone had dressed and bound his wounds. He lay beneath two woolen blankets, and the dust had been washed from his clothes.

Jason, Billy thought, turning his head to each side as he sought some sign of the young man. It was strange the way life turned. It wasn't so long ago that the boy had stood frail, seemingly defenseless in the face of Stephens's bullying.

"You can't always judge a horse by the color of his coat," Billy mumbled. That had been one of his father's favorite sayings. So much of the time it was what was inside a horse or a man that gave him substance.

"So, you're finally awake," Jason said, emerging from the trees. "'Bout time. I was worried you might sleep till next year."

"How . . . long?" Billy asked, feeling a flash of pain as he tried to flex his legs.

"Two days. Better part of a third. I did what I could. There's a doc in Trinidad, but I was afraid to fetch him. Stephens was bound to catch wind of it."

"Bound to," Billy agreed.

"Think you feel good enough to take some broth? I found a couple of chickens."

"Found?"

"Well, you know how it is with chickens. They wander sometimes, Billy."

"I hope you stole 'em from someone who could stand the loss," Billy said, wincing as he sat up. "Now, do you figure we can get me moving around some?"

"I wouldn't just yet," Jason warned. "You lost a fair amount of blood, and that hole in your leg was pretty wide."

"Can't lie here forever."

"Give it another day. Then I'll help you."

Billy nodded.

As it happened, Billy wasn't able to stir much for the balance of the week. Each time he moved even slightly, blood began to seep through the bandages, and the pain would grow severe. There was a general dizziness as well, but that began to pass as he took in solid food.

"That game seems more appealing every day I'm here," Billy remarked as he and Jason ate another rabbit. "Wish I had my rifle. We could take a deer."

"Best to lie low and rely on the snares," Jason warned. "I saw Stephens riding by the river yesterday."

"He's looking for you," Billy said. "I guess he imagines he's got a score to settle."

"He does," Jason said, smiling. "He doesn't know it yet, though. And when he does, it'll be too late."

"You took a real chance coming up here."

"No more'n you took back in the saloon for me. I've seen those three at work before, especially Stephens."

"You saved my life."

"Just returnin' the favor."

21

Billy finally got to his feet the next day, but he didn't move very far. His thigh was stiff and sore, and each movement brought fresh surges of pain. Billy'd had experience with gunshot wounds, though. He knew better than to let the muscles stiffen. He had no desire to be lame the rest of his life.

The wounds in his chest and shoulder healed faster. The flesh of his chest had begun knitting itself together already, and there was hardly any drainage from the shoulder. But despite all his efforts, the thigh continued to swell and fester.

"Got to open it again," Billy finally announced. "Must've missed some of the lead."

"Likely." Jason nodded.

"Even the surgeons do it," Billy said. "You did a fine job of binding it."

"I should've hauled you into town, got the doc to look at it."

"Got us both killed, you mean," Billy said.

"We've got a marshal."

"Oh?"

"But he's not apt to take on Stephens."

"Man's got survival instincts. May turn out he's a man to know."

On toward evening Billy heated a blade. Then Jason opened the wound. Dark fluids mixed with blood seeped from the opening. Billy felt little after the first cut. His whole leg went numb. After probing the flesh for what seemed an eternity, Jason located a fragment of lead. Then he pressed the hot blade against Billy's leg, sealing the wound.

Billy felt very little of that also. The moment the pain shot through him, he lost consciousness.

The next morning the wound was less tender, and the following day Billy accompanied Jason to the river. They spent half that day plucking rainbow trout from the water, and toward evening, they enjoyed a feast of trout and onions, with a rare can of peaches for dessert.

"That wander off the farm, too?" Billy asked.

"Fell off a shelf," Jason explained.

"Well, pickin' it up might've brought on a strain. I wouldn't want to bother a man with something like that."

"My thinkin' exactly."

"I believe you've got the makings of a bandit, Jason McNally," Billy said, laughing so hard that his wounds ached.

"I've had my chances to learn. You remember Mike Dunstan. You know how he rode down those farmers back on the Cimarron, shot down anybody who didn't do things his way. Stephens isn't much different. He robs anyone out here who's got four bits to his name."

"There are other ways to make your path in this life."

"Sellin' your services with a gun?"

"I turned away from that." Billy sighed. "No, a long time ago, just after the war, I took to the high country, up near the Bighorn Mountains. Did some placer mining."

"Pannin' for gold?"

"In the beginning. We got a bit more into it once we found some color. I always heard Colorado was gold country. Maybe we ought to follow the Purgatory a ways, see if she's holding anything worth panning."

"Others have been up there," Jason said. "Nobody ever found anything worth stayin' for."

"Then it might still be there waiting for us."

"And Stephens?"

"That's got to be tended to first," Billy said, his eyes darkening as he gazed toward town.

"But you're in no shape to challenge a man as fast with a pistol as Hart Stephens."

"Then I guess I'll have to do it another way," Billy said. "But it's got to be done."

Jason frowned, but then nodded.

Billy began his preparations by walking. At first there was more stumbling to it than anything else, but gradually the muscles in his thigh loosened and he was once again able to stand upright. There remained an unmistakable limp, but it wouldn't prevent his challenging Stephens and the others when the chosen moment arrived.

Shooting was another matter. The old long-barreled Colt he'd carried since his days in the mountains of Montana was gone. Billy had little luck with the clumsy Remington revolver Jason had brought from Trinidad.

"The sights must be off a foot and a half, and the firing pin's half gone. I'd be about as well off to carry a frying pan," Billy complained.

"I've got one of those. Could be your aim's off," Jason suggested.

"Not that much. See what twenty dollars will buy in the way of a handgun next time you sneak into town."

"And where am I going to come by twenty dollars?" Jason asked.

"It might fall off a shelf. But just in case it doesn't, here," Billy said, pulling out two ten-dollar notes seemingly from nowhere.

"Where'd you . . ."

"My belt," Billy explained. "I always figured the time might come when I got caught short. Looks like this is it."

Jason went into Trinidad that very night. He returned before dawn with an Army-issue Colt and enough shot and powder to kill a dozen men.

"Figure I need that much practice, do you?" Billy asked.

"More, but this is all I could afford. I brought my Winchester, too, just in case."

"Got shells for it?"

"Twenty or so."

"Wouldn't want you running shy like that time up on the Cimarron."

"No. I heard Loman's talkin' about leavin' soon for Denver."

"Then I guess I'd best be ready soon."

"It still seems a fool's play, Billy. The odds are all wrong. You can't take on three men."

"You wouldn't have me just walk away and let 'em get away with what they did?"

24

"Gettin' killed won't change it."

"I hadn't planned on getting myself shot again. No, we'll be playing by my rules this time around. They'll freeze a full second wonderin' if I'm a ghost. Then again I don't plan on facin' all of 'em at once."

"They don't spend a lot of hours apart."

"We'll figure it all out. I'm not proud of the time I spent with Dunstan, but I didn't spend those months without learnin' some things."

"He'd likely shoot 'em in the back."

"No, he'd set it all up so they'd shoot each other. But what we're lookin' for's the chance to separate Loman and that fancy dresser . . ."

"Brown."

". . . separate Loman and Brown from Stephens."

"But they're not apt to start anything till Stephens shows."

"They're not apt to have a choice," Billy said in a voice that chilled the air.

Most of that morning Billy practiced firing the Colt. It felt awkward even though the pistol was actually lighter than Billy's own gun. He couldn't seem to hold it steady, and his arm ached after firing only three times.

"The bleedin's started all over," Jason said, frowning as two small spots of red seeped through Billy's shirt. "Best leave it at that for today."

"No, go find me a rock, one that feels heavy in your hand."

Jason walked toward the spring, knelt down, and picked up a large chunk of limestone. He passed it over to Billy, who began raising, then lowering it.

"You're goin' to open the wounds again," Jason cautioned him.

"You're too young to sound like an old woman," Billy said. "It does it good to bleed some. Clears out the evil odors."

"That's your Comanche upbringin' talkin' again. A man's only got so much blood to lose."

25

"I've got a bit more," Billy said, laughing, as he continued lifting the rock. "Once my arm gets used to the weight, the gun'll seem second nature. That's as it should be."

Although the bleeding continued, Billy adjusted to the weight. The next morning he was able to fire all six chambers without flinching.

"You still can't hit the side of a barn, though," Jason pointed out.

"That'll come. The sights are still off."

"Must be. Otherwise Billy Starr'd shoot the eye out of a needle."

"Don't call me Starr," Billy said, staring angrily at his young friend. "I left that name behind me."

"It appears to me the name's all you left. You're turnin' back to the same life."

"Am I?" Billy asked, reloading the gun. A dozen images appeared in his mind, but he shook them away. "No, Jason, I'm not looking for a chance to prove who I am. I'm not shooting somebody on account of who they are. This is justice."

"That's what Pa called it when he shot down those farmers. He was gettin' even for them havin' Ma killed. Only how can it be justice when little girls and babies get shot?"

"I'm talking about grown men who put lead into me."

"It's all the same," Jason said, shaking his head.

"I can't walk away."

"I know," Jason said sadly. "Neither can I."

After adjusting the sights and giving the Colt a thorough cleaning, Billy began hitting his marks consistently. Following three more days of practice, he was satisfied he could hit what he aimed at.

"So, what do we do now?" Jason asked.

"We ride to town," Billy said, painfully throwing a blanket onto the back of his mustang pony. "I'll wait outside for a time. You scout the place, let me know where they are."

26

"And then?"

"We find out whether I ought to've waited another two or three weeks."

"They're goin' to kill you, Billy. You know that."

"Hah!" Billy said, laughing. "They had their chance. They'll never have a better one. No, this is my play. You'll see. The one thing I know on God's good earth is how to handle myself in a fight. Watch and see."

"I just . . ."

"What?"

"I just wish . . ."

"Wish what?"

"Oh, I don't know," Jason said, staring at the ground. "There ought to be some better way."

"Not that I know of, boy."

"Just don't let 'em kill you."

"I hadn't planned on it."

"When it's all over, we'll ride west, into the Rockies?"

"Don't see what could hold us back," Billy said.

They rode slowly, silently along the Purgatory. They moved as if no one else on the face of the earth existed. Then when the town grew near, Billy pulled his pony to a halt. Jason continued toward Trinidad.

"Good luck, Jason," Billy whispered when Jason was well beyond range of hearing him. "Keep a wary eye out for ambush."

But there were no ambushes, no obstacles of any kind. Jason made his way through town, stopping first at the livery, then at the saloon, and finally at the hotel. From the porch, he finally waved Billy into Trinidad.

"So, little horse, this is it," Billy remarked, urging the mustang into a trot. "We'll settle this once and for all."

As he rode onward, he remembered the dark parlor of the hotel in Cimarron City where he had killed Luke Hall, shot him down with hardly a whimper of disapproval from the crowded room full of people. There were other duels back in Cimarron, all of them leading to the day he had killed Texas Bob Smith, shot him down before Dunstan's eyes, then blew Dunstan's toe off for good measure.

"I was a fool to think there was any peace in this life," Billy said, watching Jason's red-streaked eyes as the pony approached the hotel. "There isn't any."

CHAPTER 5

Few in Trinidad who watched Billy Cook ride into town that morning took notice. If they failed to bother themselves with a dark-eyed stranger wearing a bloodstained shirt, they might be forgiven. It was a commonplace enough sight in a land haunted by renegade Indians, outlaws come west from the Nations or north from New Mexico, or drifting miners and gamblers down on their luck.

Few who saw what followed quickly forgot those eyes or the man who stepped down from his horse and entered the lobby of the Trinidad Hotel.

"It's just like you planned, Billy," Jason whispered at the doorway. "Stephens is over at the saloon. Loman's in the parlor, havin' himself some breakfast. Brown's still upstairs."

"Watch the back door," Billy said. "See that no one comes in or out."

"Done," Jason said, cradling the Winchester rifle he'd been careful to conceal before. "Don't let 'em get you, Billy."

"I won't."

But even before Billy could turn toward the parlor, the plan went awry. Brown appeared on the stairs, spotted Jason, and began to speak.

"Well, now, lookee here," Brown said. "It's our little friend from the saloon. Hey, Loman, look who's . . ."

Billy turned at that moment, and all the color raced from Brown's face.

"Can't . . . be," the gambler stammered. "You're . . . dead."

"No, you are," Billy said, fingering the handle of his pistol. "Anytime you care to say, Brown."

"This is crazy," Brown said, turning toward the hotel clerk and the scattered guests who occupied the lobby. "I'm no gunfighter."

"I'm giving you more of a chance than you gave me out on that hillside, mister," Billy said angrily. "Come on. It's time to settle up."

"Look, it wasn't my idea," Brown pleaded. "I've got your money. What was it, three hundred? Look, here's three, four hundred. Gold."

Brown produced a pouch filled with gold pieces. He tossed it onto the floor, and Jason bent over to pick it up.

"There's the matter of a hat, too," Billy said.

"Upstairs," Brown said, wiping sweat from his forehead. "The boots and pistol are there as well. Loman sold the coat, but it's still at the mercantile. You can buy it back."

"I can?" Billy asked, his eyes darkening.

"I'll do it. Just let me run over there. It won't take a minute."

"I'd be less than likely to turn my back on you a second time," Billy said, gazing at Brown with cold eyes.

"And what about me?" Loman's voice boomed out.

Billy made a half turn so that he could face both Brown and the teamster. Loman's bulky figure broke through the other guests.

"I thought for sure we'd left you for the worms," Loman said, laughing. "I knew I should've made sure. Oh, well, I won't make that mistake again."

"You won't be making any mistake, period. Not ever again," Billy said. "You I want most of all, Loman."

"Somebody fetch the marshal," the clerk said, nervously backing up as Loman stepped closer to Billy.

"Seems to me these gentlemen have a score to settle," one of the guests said. "Marshal'd only delay things, make 'em tend to it out of town. Wouldn't make much difference as I see it."

The others nodded, and the clerk knelt behind the front desk.

"So, who's it going to be first?" Billy asked.

"I watched you play cards, mister," Brown said, laughing now. "You love to run a bluff by. If you'd meant to shoot us, you'd done it by now. I saw your shoulder before. It's bleeding even now. You'd be lucky to hold a pistol, much less use one."

"Willin' to bet your life on that, are you?" Billy asked.

Brown regained his nervousness, but Loman was unimpressed.

"Can't be long before Hart Stephens'll be in," Loman said. "We eat breakfast together. Even if you could take one or even both of us, there's no way on this earth you'll outdraw Hart."

"Watch the door, Jason," Billy whispered. "Now, let's have a full accounting. Loman, I believe you've got a coat of mine."

"I told you it's at the mercantile," Brown said.

"I wasn't talking to you," Billy said. "Loman, you send someone over there to get it."

"Choke on it," Loman said. "I'm not about to do a thing just 'cause you said to do it."

"That's a shame because I'd about decided to let you have a chance at life," Billy told them. "Now it's got to go the whole mile, doesn't it?"

"I paid you," Brown said, pointing at the bag of coins in Jason's hand. "You settle anything else with Stephens. It was his idea to shoot you."

"I'll be tending to him . . . a bit later," Billy said. "But I

31

left you two behind me once before. I paid a high price for the bit of education I got. I'll not pay twice."

"But . . ." Brown began.

It was then that Loman produced a small pistol from his sleeve. He fired, but the ball struck a lamp beside Billy's head. Billy never wavered. Even as Loman pulled back the hammer for a second try, Billy's Colt discharged, sending a single ball across the lobby of the hotel. Loman clutched his face as the shot smashed his cheekbone and splintered his jaw. The teamster's mouth hung open, and he died without speaking whatever was on the tip of his tongue.

"Loman?" Brown cried out, drawing a knife and charging at Billy.

"Look out!" Jason yelled.

Billy turned quickly, lifted his knee, and Brown fell downward, rolling across the carpet until he came to a rest beside a small reading table.

"You . . . had . . . the money," Brown said, gasping.

Billy glanced at the pouch as Jason handed it over. Brown sat up. Only then could the knife be seen, driven to the hilt through Brown's side. The gambler's eyes grew hazy, and then he fell.

"Summon the marshal!" the clerk screamed. "Mr. Brown's been murdered."

"Was Brown pulled the knife himself," one of the by-standers declared. "As for Loman, he drew first. A man's got a right to defend his interests and especially his life."

Billy leaned against the doorway and returned the coin pouch to Jason.

"This is no time to pass out, Billy," Jason warned.

"Go upstairs, fetch my gun, boots, and hat," Billy said, groaning as pain from his thigh worked its way through him.

"But Stephens . . ."

"I'll see if I can locate him," Billy said, turning and stumbling through the twin doors of the hotel.

Through the residue of powder smoke that drifted from the hotel lobby, Billy detected a single rider making a hasty departure from the southern end of town.

Billy raised the Colt, then lowered it. Maybe he would have chanced such a shot with his own pistol, but there was no hope of hitting a horseman from two hundred yards with this one, and the street was busy with children chasing a prairie chicken.

Billy restored the pistol to its holster, then slumped against the hard pine bench that stood on the porch. While Jason sought out Billy's hat and other possessions, Billy himself did his best to tighten the bindings on his thigh and shoulder, thus lessening the bleeding.

"What in blue blazes is goin' on over here?" a deep voice bellowed out.

Billy wearily turned toward a tall man wearing a heavy black overcoat. A five-pointed star was pinned to the coat.

"I shot a man," Billy said, pointing toward the door of the hotel. "Another fell on a knife he drew and got himself killed."

"Who the devil are you?" the marshal asked, looking Billy over. "You ever been in Trinidad before?"

"Just once," Billy said. "Long enough to play a little cards with a fellow named Stephens and another couple who used to go by the names of Loman and Brown."

"Those the ones you killed?"

"I only killed one," Billy said. "Loman. Brown did the trick himself."

"I don't suppose he cut himself shavin', though. Way I figure things, you were the cause of both of 'em bein' dead."

"Or they were, dependin' on your point of view," Billy said. "See these holes in me," he added, pointing out the wounds. "They shot me from an ambush out past the river. Left me for dead."

"Sounds like Loman," the marshal agreed. "Never thought Brown had that much sass. Stephens, though, he's more one to face a man head-on. 'Less he figured you were the one with the upper hand. What was it you called yourself, mister?"

"Cook. Billy Cook."

"And you hail from?"

"Here and there. Lately from Denver."

"Not from the Nations? Cimarron, maybe?"

"Once."

"Well, Mr. Cook, we don't care too much for disturbances in Trinidad. I'd look upon it with favor if you'd clear up whatever business you might have here this afternoon and be gone by nightfall."

"Doesn't sound like I'm too welcome."

"I'd hate to put out a warrant on you, Cook. It takes so long to get word to Denver, and it costs money to get a judge down here, even more to pay a jury and a hangman. It's a bother. Still, if you were to stay here long . . ."

"I don't generally like towns," Billy said, frowning. "I expect we'll be heading out after we get something to eat."

"Now that's what I'd call fine thinkin'," the marshal said, nodding twice.

Jason appeared with Billy's things then, and Billy rose shakily.

"Just one thing left," Billy said, stepping toward the mercantile.

"I don't suppose we'll be havin' the pleasure of your company in the future?" the marshal asked.

"I believe the sooner I see the last of this place the better."

The marshal nodded again, then stepped to one side as Billy limped across the street. After redeeming his coat, Billy followed Jason to the cantina. As they enjoyed their meal, beef bits cooked in red peppers, Billy emptied the contents of Brown's pouch.

"Barely fifty dollars," Jason said with a scowl.

"Not surprisin'," Billy grumbled. "That man had the most dishonest eyes I ever saw."

"I should've gone through his pockets."

"And got yourself locked up? No, we should've settled accounts beforehand. Now it's too late."

"Fifty dollars isn't much of a stake."

"Well, it'll buy powder, some flour, salt, warm blankets. We'll need a couple of flat-bottomed pans, too. Tin if you can find 'em."

"There's no shortage of minin' supplies in this town," Jason said, laughing. "I'd better get you a shirt and a new pair of trousers. The ones you've got on are a bit full of holes."

"Guess so," Billy said, smiling faintly.

"Are we goin' on into the high country, or do you plan to follow Stephens?"

"Couldn't do much about him now if I wanted to," Billy admitted. "No, it's time I put this behind me. If we're lucky, Stephens won't stop till he crosses the Mexican border. Maybe some Apache'll take a liking to his scalp."

"That'd be too easy," Jason said. "Nothin' in my life's been easy. No, I figure we'll cross paths with Hart Stephens again."

"Well, as long as it's a bit later, I don't care. I'm ready to climb a mountain and find me a place to lie down and sleep for about a month."

"Winter's comin'," Jason reminded him. "We'll have need of a cabin. There's meat to be put by."

"Never any rest for an old campaigner." Billy sighed, remembering what his colonel had said after Gettysburg. "There's always another battle to be fought."

CHAPTER 6

After rounding up the necessary supplies, Billy led the way westward along the north bank of the Purgatory River. Jason trailed a few feet behind, humming old cattle songs or chattering away about the shapes of clouds. As Billy gazed at the lonely peaks towering in the distance, though, he felt as if no one else existed on the face of the earth.

Past Trinidad, the valley was mostly deserted. The riverbed provided a good path for a time, but after a few miles the Purgatory spilled over its banks. Billy turned from the river and wove through the tall aspens and spruces on the hillside.

"From here on I guess we make our own way," Jason said.

I always have, Billy thought as they continued. It was one of those special abilities of his, finding a route through the hills, vanishing into the woods when he chose. It had served him well in the scattered fighting across the wilderness of northern Virginia.

"There's something about mountains," Billy said as they

gazed at the hulking Spanish Peaks. "Takes a man away from his worries."

"Maybe," Jason said, sighing. "I remember Pa sayin' something like that when we came down from Kansas to the Cimarron. It was goin' to be a new beginning for us. We would have all the land we ever wanted and more cattle than a man could count in a whole year."

"It helps to have a dream."

"It came true—for a while. Then we started havin' trouble with the farmers. Dunstan came and—"

"Something always comes along to change things."

"What changed things for you, Billy?" Jason asked.

For a moment Billy stared off into the distance. His lip quivered, and his palms grew moist. He took off his hat and pushed back tangles of dirty blond hair from his forehead.

"I don't entirely know," he finally admitted.

"The war?"

Billy studied the hat. The C.S.A. insignia was still there, but the shine on it had long since given way after a decade of skirmishes. Those years had brought pain. Billy had spent them on the run, first from the Yanks, then Sioux horsemen, later mostly from himself and the violence that had become a way of life.

"Two of my uncles died at Sharpsburg," Jason said sadly. "Ma used to worry about the war goin' on till John and I got in it."

"That brother of yours is a mean one."

"He never was the same after the Yanks burned us out back in Carolina. You could see him change. Before that he always kind of looked after me. Once he took to shootin' off that pistol of his, he had no use for anyone."

"Well, I expect by now he's learned what reward waits for a man who straps on a Colt and tests his hand against others."

"I haven't heard a word of Pa since I left the ranch. Is he well?"

"I left the same night you did, Jason. Didn't see your pa

37

again, but I didn't hear he'd come to any harm. He was still raiding farms till a U.S. marshal came down."

Jason glanced toward the ground, and Billy frowned.

"It's hard losing a wife," Billy said. "I suppose sometimes life swallows a man up, makes him so bitter he can't help but strike out at anything he sees."

"He was different before."

"So you told me, Jason. He could be changed again, you know. Ever thought of going back?"

"Too many memories," Jason said, sighing. "Anyway, John's there. Pa always took John more to his heart than me. I knew a long time ago I'd be movin' on. Shoot, I'm nearly eighteen."

"I guess that's as good an age to be a man as another."

"I've killed men. I close to got killed myself, twice! If you hadn't stepped in back at the saloon, Stephens would've shot me. Wasn't the first time you took my side. There was that ambush back on the Cimarron. Then at the ranch."

Billy slapped the dust from his hat and returned it to his head.

"I'd say that was all evened out now." Billy nudged his horse forward.

"Then maybe we can be real partners. Who knows? There could be a fortune in gold just waitin' for us up there in those mountains," Jason said, trying to keep the conversation rolling. But Billy's thoughts were miles away, and soon the two dusty horsemen rode onward in silence.

They continued, mile after mile. Sometimes Billy whistled some old battle tune along with Jason, a lingering hymn of lost campaigns. Mostly he listened to the seventeen-year-old gab about hawks and buzzards and the way the leaves on the aspens had changed from burnt orange to bright scarlet.

It was a time of peace; an idyllic paradise that offered a momentary refuge from painful memories.

What's it been now? Billy asked himself as they made camp that night. Ten years? A decade of fighting, first against the Yanks, then against the hazards of cattle trails

38

and mountain winters. And last of all the cold-eyed, dark-hearted strangers who would have ended both the pain and the joy so easily.

Eighteen, Billy thought, watching as Jason emptied a tin of beans in the skillet, then mixed in some bits of dried beef. By eighteen Billy'd close to thrown Grant into the Tennessee River, led his company at Sharpsburg, stood off the bluecoats at Fredericksburg, crashed Hooker's line from the woods at Chancellorsville, and half died when Pickett's thousands had been slaughtered in Pennsylvania.

I was eighteen when they took me for the cavalry, he remembered. And I wasn't even twenty when General Lee surrendered.

"Food's 'bout ready," Jason called from the small campfire he'd built. "Takes forever to get anything done up here."

"That's the way it is in the high country," Billy said, turning away from his memories. "Should've told you to use the pine. It catches faster. Then you can add the hard woods."

"How much longer till we reach gold country?" Jason asked, stirring the strange concoction in the skillet.

"Could be we're there already. But these slopes'll prove impossible come winter. If the snows don't smother you, the winds'll sweep you away. We need to find a valley of some kind, a place that doesn't catch the full force of the weather."

"Figure there'll be such a place?"

"Always has been before," Billy said, accepting a platter of beef and beans from Jason. "Besides, it'd be better to be a few miles from Trinidad. Just in case."

"Just in case?" Jason asked between bites.

"Lots of renegades ride along that road to Santa Fe. Wouldn't do to pan all winter, dig all spring, then get robbed all summer."

"I don't guess they'd have a lot of success tanglin' with us."

"Can't work a claim and guard the hills at the same time. Got to sleep now and then."

"So we keep goin'?"

"Three more days, a week at the outside."

"Sounds easy enough."

"Does it?" Billy asked, smiling grimly as he studied the adventuresome sparkle in Jason's eyes. "Winter's not so far away. Comes early in the high country."

"And?"

"We've got a fair ridge yet to cross, and we'll have need of a good cabin, lots of wood, meat to put up before the passes freeze and the game scatters."

"But we'll get on." Jason scraped the last bit of beef off the tin plate and into his mouth.

"Maybe," Billy said. "Know how old I was the first time I took off for the hills, Jason?"

"No." The young man looked up as Billy leaned against a pine tree and reminisced.

"Fourteen, I think. Spent the best part of a year with Comanches. But when I came back, Papa was glad to see me. I was off to the war before I'd turned sixteen. Didn't have much to come back to after that. But I tell you, Jason, if I had, I'd have stuck myself into the ground, and it'd have taken a cyclone to pull me off there."

"You worried I won't pull my weight?"

"Didn't say that."

"I might not be a match for Hart Stephens, but I did manage to fend for myself half a year in Trinidad before you happened along," Jason said.

"Never doubted it."

"Then why don't you want me to stay with you? I can cook. I'll do my part of the work once I know how."

Billy frowned as he saw the damage his words had done. Young Jason's face was as red as a Colorado sunrise. It wasn't what he'd intended.

"Wasn't me I was thinking about," Billy said. "Was you. It'd be a comfort to have somebody to split the work, to share the worst of the winter's loneliness. But it's hard up there in the high country, and it's harder not knowin' what's come of your family. I know. And I know something else. If you don't go back now, you never will."

"I never will," Jason declared. "I knew that when I rode off that first night. I don't belong with Pa and John. Maybe I never did. A man doesn't have to be thirty to know when it's time to head out."

"Thirty?" Billy said, laughing. "How old you figure I am?"

"Never thought about it. You as young as thirty?"

"This is what, eighteen hundred and seventy-one? That'd make me twenty-five."

"Twenty-five?" Jason gasped.

"The years alone don't age a man, Jason. I've probably got a scar or a broken bone for each one of those years. Thirty can be a full life for a man in the high country."

"Twenty can be a lifetime for a gunfighter. Or ten for a farmer back on the Cimarron."

Billy shared Jason's frown as they both remembered the farms Jason's father had raided; the men, women, and children who had been killed.

"I mean to put all that behind me," Jason said finally. "I may never forget, but maybe . . ."

"Sure," Billy said, nodding. "Maybe we can find something better."

Billy supposed it was that dream of something better that always drove men to climb the next ridge, to explore the valley below, or to venture into the deep forests beyond. Certainly it was what prompted him and Jason McNally to continue their quest. Hours of threading their way along the river jostled them from head to toe, and more than once Billy noticed a bit of blood leaking from his wounds. But the chill air kept back the fever that might have struck in July, and the journey was never halted for more than a few hours in spite of Jason's objections.

"A dead partner would do me little good," Jason complained.

"If three men with rifles couldn't kill me, no bunch of

rocks and pine trees's going to do it," Billy declared. And the ride was resumed.

Three days out of Trinidad they made camp at a bend of the Purgatory. The sun had been bright and the air crisp, so after ten miles, Billy had signaled a halt.

"I'm tired of beans and dried beef," Billy announced.

"I've got some salt pork," Jason said.

"If you've got the patience, I think we might do better," Billy said, drawing from his saddlebags a spool of line and a cork holding a dozen iron fishhooks. "Trout taste particularly fine this time a year."

Jason climbed down from his horse immediately, and Billy followed his partner to the river. After tying line to aspen poles and attaching hooks baited with unfortunate crickets, they abandoned their boots, rolled up their trousers, and waded into the river.

"Sure it's only autumn?" Jason asked through chattering teeth as the frigid chill of the stream attacked his bare legs.

"Winter'll be here soon enough," Billy agreed. "But fried trout's a fair tonic for a cold stream."

The thought brought growls from their stomachs, and the better part of the afternoon was passed in the effort to lure rainbow trout from their hiding places amidst the rocks of the river.

By dusk seven beautiful trout had been collected, and while Jason cleaned the fish, Billy built a small fire. He started with bunches of dry grass, then added pine branches splintered by an ax. Later aspen was added so that a steady, if hesitant, flame appeared.

After dinner Billy led the way on foot up the mountain. As the sun disappeared into the distant slopes, it seemed as if they were truly atop the entire universe. Land spread out below as far as the eye could see. The air was clear, though thin, and in spite of the cold, Billy grew warm.

"I feel like I own the whole world," Jason declared. "You figure anyone else's ever been up here?"

"Cheyenne used to hunt here. Ute before that. Arapaho. Not too many white men."

42

"I feel so at peace, Billy."

"That's the way it is in the high country. Sometimes you get lucky and it stays that way."

"You said you were in the Rockies once before. You didn't stay, though."

"I was in the Powder River country. Dug for gold then, too. Sioux didn't want us up there. They took to killing anybody they could find. Rode down a whole army of bluecoats in sixty-eight."

"So you left?"

"After the army quit, there wasn't much hope of staying. Best land was played out, so I drifted south."

"That's how it is out west. If it's not the Yank cavalry after you, it's the Indians."

"Got to remember, Jason. The Indians were here first," Billy said, resting back in the soft meadow grass and staring at the darkening sky overhead. "White men brought 'em awful grief."

"You told me you knew Comanche."

"Lived with 'em for a time. They were different, but they had their honor, like any good man. You could get along with 'em if you understood what they were after. You can with anybody, I suppose."

"Then how come there've been so many wars? How come Pa and the farmers back on the Cimarron took to shootin' each other?"

"I guess sometimes nobody really takes the time to see th' other side of things. Or maybe they just don't care."

"Billy?"

"Yeah?"

"Do you sometimes miss not havin' a family? Ever wish you were back home again?"

"No," Billy said, gazing once again at the shadowy mountains to the west. Not sometimes! Always.

As they returned to the dying embers of their campfire, Billy saw two scarlet leaves fall from a nearby aspen.

That's me, he thought. I'm just like that, a leaf drifting in the autumn wind, waiting for the end to come. But he

43

kept the thought to himself. Jason was still filled with the fire that an adventure newly begun brings to a young man.

And me? Billy asked himself. I ride on along, dreaming of something better than there will be, wondering if I can dodge the next peril, knowing it will always be the same. I'm just a leaf. . . .

CHAPTER 7

The Purgatory, as all rivers do, grew narrow and more turbulent as Billy and Jason neared its source high in the broad slopes of the Spanish Peaks. The ground became more and more rocky, and what path there was between the tall pines and spruces was often blocked by great boulders as tall as a man. More often than not Billy led the way on foot, leading his weary horse behind him. In spite of land made slippery from the almost constant rains, they made progress. Rock slides often swept away whole hillsides, though, forcing the two wayfarers to bend their path accordingly.

There was a fierce chill to the air now, even during the heart of the day. At night Billy huddled in his blankets and hoped that soon a suitable valley would appear so that a winter home might be carved from the pines before the first snows arrived.

"Winter comes early at this height," Billy said over and over. "Best to be prepared."

But each time a seemingly suitable place presented itself, he would study the river and pronounce it too swift.

Or else there wouldn't be enough wood for a cabin, or game would be scarce.

"We've got to stop sometime," Jason complained.

But Billy would only frown and shake his head.

"I'll know the proper site when I see it," he'd say, then lead his horse onward.

"Don't see how one place is so much different from another," Jason grumbled as they climbed higher and higher into the peaks.

Billy knew the difference, though. To be a true refuge a place had to be atop the world, safe from the greedy fingers of teamsters and miners, distant from the hungry eyes of the town builders and civilizers, protected from the scavenging bands of killers who swooped down on isolated cabins, robbing and slaying.

It wasn't possible to put into words the wariness Billy felt as they wove their way through the steep slopes of the Rockies. But he supposed Jason knew, or perhaps understood some bit of it. Once as they sighted a party of horsemen along the river below, Billy motioned his companion into the trees, only to discover that Jason was already dragging his reluctant horse behind a boulder.

The two of them hid among the pines half a day, readying themselves for a possible confrontation. But the strangers stayed with the river, and Billy sighed with relief when he saw they were following the Purgatory downriver, out of the mountains toward Trinidad and the rolling buffalo valleys below.

"Only a fool heads into the mountains so late in the year," Billy observed. "Most folks winter in towns."

"Only a fool?" Jason asked.

"Only a fool or a man grown weary of his neighbors," Billy said, laughing. "And me, well, I'm tired of people in general, neighbor or not."

Jason nodded his agreement, and the two continued their journey.

Now that they were nearing the timberline, Billy eased the daily pace. Neither he and Jason nor the horses could manage much more than five miles per day. Already the

46

thin air left them gasping at the conclusion of the simplest climb, and often it seemed to Billy that his lungs were aflame. The horses coughed and shivered. Only Jason seemed immune from the miseries of the altitude.

The young can endure anything, Billy thought as he led the way to an outcropping of stone on the hillside above. By late afternoon they'd made a camp of sorts under the overhanging rock. The mountainside afforded some protection from the harsh northerly winds, and by spreading pine needles along the rock wall, a place of some comfort was made.

"This wouldn't make a bad place to winter," Jason said as he took a bit of jerked beef from his pocket. "Lots of tall pine for a cabin."

"Next valley, maybe," Billy said, taking the long Winchester rifle Jason had located among Loman's belongings and holding it fondly in his hands. "I've got my mind on fresh meat just now. I saw deer tracks down by the river. Care to make a scout with me?"

"I could do with a bit of venison," Jason said, stuffing the remains of the jerky back in his pocket. "Let's go."

"Don't you suppose you'd be a lot more use with a rifle?" Billy said, laughing as he pointed to Jason's Winchester.

"You don't mean to say you need help shootin', do you?" Jason asked.

"I wasn't just bringing you along for the pleasure of your company, you know."

"Well, I thought you likely were," Jason said, cracking a smile. "Wouldn't be much use to you otherwise. Unless you get yourself shot again."

"You keep yapping, Jason McNally, every deer from here to Pikes Peak'll be on the run."

Jason laughed once more, then picked up his rifle and followed Billy down the mountainside. Soon the two of them were turning a large half circle past the edge of the river where Billy had spotted the tracks.

"Shouldn't we track 'em?" Jason asked quietly.

"You run as fast as a deer?" Billy said, pausing a moment. "I don't. What you have to do is think like a deer. They come down to the river for a drink, but there's not much to eat there. They'd likely be back in some thicket for now. So we'll slip back around, keeping the wind on our faces. That way they can't smell us."

"I've hunted before."

"Good. Then you know mostly it's getting to a shot, not hitting it. I went after my first antlers when I wasn't as high as a horse's tail. Learned from the Comanche. My papa and I used to set off with old Yellow Shirt every fall to hunt the meadows along the Brazos."

"That's the chief you told me about back at Pa's ranch. His son's the one who cut your arm."

"That's right," Billy said, rubbing the old scar. "Red Wolf, he called himself."

"Suppose he's still alive?"

"No," Billy said, sighing. "Saw him dead. All the old ones are gone now: Papa, Yellow Shirt, Henry King. Ole Henry, he fought Santa Anna at San Jacinto, then again in Mexico."

"How come you didn't go back there, Billy?"

"Did once," Billy said, frowning. "After the war. Found out I didn't belong anymore. It's hard, finding that out."

"I know," Jason said, slipping past Billy and leading the way out beyond the river.

They spoke no more about leaving home, or anything else for that matter. Hunting was serious business for such men. It meant filling one's belly or starving, and a weakened man had little hope of challenging the Rocky Mountains in winter. Billy had no more words to share, anyway. Thoughts of his home, of the little house along the great river, always brought pain.

What about it, Billy? he asked himself. Why don't you head back there, try to patch up the holes in your life?

It often tempted him. But always he recalled the hard words of his brother, words that had offered no hope of reconciliation, of peace between them. It wasn't my doing, Billy told himself. But we're both Papa's sons, and I could never be the one to draw a gun on my own family. So Sam had taken the ranch, the livestock, and the family name. Billy, well, he'd taken the long, hard road, first north, then west, next south and east, finally west again.

It's the same road, though, Billy thought as he spied the buck. The same road leading nowhere.

Jason had seen the deer, too. From the size of its antlers, Billy knew it'd seen many winters in the high Rockies. Beside the big buck were four smaller animals, two does and a younger buck. Billy pointed to the smaller buck, but Jason frowned. Clearly the younger man wished to shoot the big one.

"Too much meat," Billy whispered as he reached Jason's side. "Take the smaller."

"But . . ." Jason started to argue.

Billy motioned toward the small meadow that spread out in front of them. The nearest doe raised her head in alarm. Billy nodded his head and flashed a look of urgency at his partner. Jason fired once, twice, a third time. But the deer had bolted. Each shot tore harmlessly through the air.

Billy raised the long-barreled Winchester to his shoulder and fixed the smaller buck in his sights. For an instant he hesitated, feeling the cold steel of the trigger send a shudder through his chest. Then he fired and the shot slammed the buck down, drove through the shoulder and into its heart.

"Good shot, Billy," Jason declared, rising to his feet.

"Not much challenge for a man with a good rifle," Billy said, remembering the old days when he and Red Wolf had used first a bow, then one of those clumsy Mexican War muskets Billy's father had brought back to the ranch in '49.

"I knew you didn't need me to do any shootin'," Jason said as they stepped toward the fallen deer.

"Might be wise if you put in some practice, Jace," Billy said, slapping the young man on the shoulder. "I wouldn't feel quite as good about things if that had been a grizzly."

"Or Hart Stephens and his bunch."

"I expect he's down in Mexico, huddled up around a bottle of bad whiskey and a pretty little *señorita*. Come to think on it, that doesn't sound like a half-bad way to pass a winter."

"No," Jason said, smiling.

"But up here on a mountaintop," Billy said, waving his hand in a circle at the tall Spanish Peaks, the majestic pines and spruces, the roiling Purgatory River. "Here a man's on top of the world. Shoshonis believe the world was born on a mountaintop, and I read somewhere the Greeks or some such did, too. Up here a man feels new, better."

"I don't," Jason said.

"You have to let the old sadness flow out of you," Billy said, cutting the deer's throat so that the blood could flow from the carcass.

"Have you?" Jason asked.

"Yes," Billy said, gazing at the clear blue sky. But as he began skinning the animal, he thought, it always comes back, though. No matter how fast or how far you run.

That night, as darkness settled in all around them, Billy and Jason continued cooking the strips of venison they'd cut from the dead buck that afternoon. Dried meat, with a bit of salt added, could last all winter. The hide was stretched out on a frame of aspen branches beside the fire.

"Wish we'd baked up some biscuits," Jason said, chewing a piece of meat.

"You'll be glad you saved that flour come winter," Billy told him.

"Seems to me winter's here already," Jason complained. "Look at that sky! It's dark as tar."

"Storm's brewing," Billy said. "But it's early for snow."

"Snows come early up here. You said so yourself."

"Still feels early," Billy said, tearing off a corner from one of the venison steaks and biting into it.

"Takes forever to cook in this high country. We'd be through by now on the plains."

"Might have company, too," Billy said between bites.

"Wouldn't mind if some of that company was from the Lily House up in Pueblo."

"Oh, you know about that place, do you?"

"I didn't land in Trinidad right off, Billy," Jason said,

laughing. "I'll bet one of those French redheads could take the chill off the night air."

"How old you say you were?" Billy asked, gazing at his friend's face in the dim light of the campfire.

"Be eighteen a little before Christmas."

"Eighteen," Billy said, sighing. "Bawdy houses and gamblers' dens. Your mama'd have a fit! She would have wanted you waltzing 'round a Richmond mansion, some little gal in a lace dress on your arm."

"Yeah," Jason said, sighing. "Not too many girls out here wear lace."

"Not too many girls out here at all, and that's a fact, Jace. By the time a female's fourteen, she's a woman, most often married or close to it. Man who's kept a daughter that long's ready to pass on the responsibility, and there're plenty of men willing and able to take her."

"Ever been married, Billy?" Jason asked.

"Close."

"Back in Texas?"

"Yes," Billy said sadly. "Up in the Powder River country, too. If I'd stayed around the Cimarron a little longer, I might have taken Jessica Hart to the altar."

"But you always leave, huh?"

"Always," Billy said, finishing the venison steak.

When the cooking was done and the meat was all salted and hung out to dry, Billy spread out his blankets and fought to get some sleep. The air was frigid, and the wind howled through the rocks like a wounded wolf.

It's cold, Billy thought, feeling icy fingers reaching through his skin and penetrating his chest. Cold as death. He remembered the feel of the Winchester's trigger.

Once, a long time ago, he'd sat in the rain, listening to the Methodist circuit rider tell of life and death and the consequences of right and wrong. That preacher seemed to be gazing right at him, telling how beautiful and peaceful heaven would be. Hell, though, was full of blazing infernos and dreadful beasts.

No, hell has no fires, Billy said to himself. It's cold . . .

a man lying alone on a mountainside, snow slowly choking off his breath.

For the first time Billy noticed how heavy the air had become. The sky overhead had swallowed the stars. It was like that terrifying night before the first day at Shiloh, close to ten years ago, when a thin-faced boy of sixteen had stood the watch, waiting for the world to change the next morning. It had, too, Billy thought. Of all the good that had touched his life, most of it was shut out forever by the clamor of cannons on that next day, by the blood and the killing, by the pain and the terrible loss.

Yes, it's cold, Billy told himself. And sometimes it seemed as if it always had been.

CHAPTER 8

The storm began as a eerie song carried on a midnight wind. Softly it brushed the mountainside with flurries of white. At first Billy failed to take notice. The snow felt like the touch of a feather. Only later, when the cold bite of the wind penetrated into his bones, did he rise from his blankets.

Oh, God, he thought, staring out at the white haze that was choking the mountains.

He'd seen autumn blizzards before, been lulled into thinking them no more than a bit of snow. Already the wind had commenced its howling and the rocks of the ledge shuddered.

"Get up!" Billy shouted to Jason McNally. "We're in trouble!"

"Trouble?" Jason asked, rubbing the sleep from his eyes.

"Snowstorm," Billy said, dragging his blankets deeper within the overhang. "Quick, bring in the horses and the gear. I've got to make us a shelter."

"A shelter?" Jason asked, reluctant to leave the warmth of the blankets.

"Yes," Billy said. "Get going. Now!"

Jason's eyes lost their drowsiness as they read the hint of panic on Billy's face. By the time Billy had grabbed his ax and set forth into the pines, Jason was already leading the hobbled horses toward the shelter of the outcropping.

That next hour Billy worked feverishly, first to fell two small pines, then to make a thatch of branches. He brought this framework to the overhang and leaned it against the rocks to make a skeleton wall.

"Gather up small branches, pine needles, anything you can find," Billy told Jason. "Weave them into the branches. That will break the bite of the wind and hold back the snow."

"The rocks will keep back the snow," Jason said, pointing to where the swirling wind blew the flakes away from the outcropping.

"For now," Billy said, heading back toward the trees to build a second frame. "Not later."

By the time Billy had added the second wall of their shelter, the wind was blasting snowdrifts toward the rock walls of the overhang. Perhaps two inches had fallen in during the first three hours. Now that much seemed to fall each minute. The horses whinnied in discomfort, but there was nothing that could be done for them. Billy and Jason huddled in their makeshift hut, walled in on two sides by rock, shielded on the others from the biting wind by Billy's thatched walls.

"It's not a cabin, but it'll do," Jason said, huddling in his blankets by the far wall.

"I'd be happier in a cave," Billy said, looking through the gaps in the branches as the snow drifted higher against the little wall. "I've seen men freeze to death in a storm like this. Men clothed in buffalo hides and sheepskin boots. Joe Tolliver for one, and he was born to the high country."

"We'll be all right."

"What makes you think that? There's no room for a fire,

and we've got little water. What meat we have'll soon freeze. I've known storms like this to blow for half a week. Then, too, there's the snow."

"Oh?"

"Snow comes deep in this country. Two, sometimes three feet at a time. We could find ourselves frozen in our own tomb up here. Then we'll starve slow, if the cold doesn't take us first."

"That's a pleasin' thought."

"Wish you'd gone home when you had the chance?"

"No," Jason said, sighing. "I always wanted to see the high mountains in winter."

"Could be you'll have the chance," Billy said. But as the fury of the wind and the chill of the earth rattled their frail shelter and drove splinters of cold through their chests, he began to doubt they'd see anything past morning.

The cold grew increasingly worse, and Billy put on every scrap of clothing he possessed. Jason did likewise. Then the two companions nestled in their woolen blankets against the hard rock wall and fought to sleep. Billy felt his knees shake and his teeth chatter as the cold ate its way ever deeper inside his chest. Breathing grew painful. His head ached.

Beside him Jason trembled like the last leaf on a cottonwood during the first week of winter, hanging on to life by the thinnest of threads, refusing to surrender. Billy himself was little better.

It's Petersburg all over again, Billy thought, remembering that dreadful winter of '64 when he'd sat in the trenches with the rest of what remained of his regiment, a tired nineteen-year-old commanding seventy horseless cavalrymen. In September they'd been six score. First sickness, then hunger, and now the cold crept in to steal away his little command.

"They ought to make you a colonel," Travis Cobb had complained. "You command a regiment, don't you?"

"Only 'cause the colonel fell. Lucky they don't make

me a sergeant. By spring there won't be enough of us left to make up a corporal's guard."

"Wouldn't be so bad if we had horses."

"We could raid then," Billy'd said, smelling the boiling pots of coffee and beef stew drifting from the Yank camps a hundred yards away. He looked off to the north into the rolling fog that marked the James River. Beyond that was Richmond, the capital. The city was starving, too, he'd heard. People there were eating their dogs.

"No worse'n having to eat your own mount," one of the men had grumbled. "Poor ole Lucifer. He carried me through many a campaign with nary a scar."

"It's just as well," Billy had said. "I hate to watch a horse suffer. There's no forage here. They'd all have starved in another week."

So the horses had been put to good use. A pair of cobblers had fashioned boots from the hides, and every bit of meat had been boiled and eaten.

At least we had fires at Petersburg, Billy thought. True, no farmer north of Reams' Station had a fence rail standing, but even on the darkest February morning, Billy'd been able to warm his hands. Now, with the cold taking possession of his fingers and toes, he longed for a few coals, a hint of warmth.

The cold, Billy told himself, was the bitterest of enemies. The creeping death, the soldiers at Petersburg had called it. Always death came in the night, unseen, leaving new corpses to be discovered in the dawn's amber glow.

I should have made the shelter earlier, should have sensed the storm. A man born to the Brazos can taste rain, read snow in the sky. There would have been time to wall in half the overhang, to make a hole for the smoke to escape. A fire . . . That would have made all the difference. A man born to the Brazos . . .

It's been a long time since you rode along the Brazos, a distant voice whispered in Billy's mind. He closed his eyes and a phantom appeared, dreamlike, a vision of beauty with soft yellow hair and long, graceful fingers that felt like velvet.

For a wonderful hour he floated through time, returned to his childhood. There he'd lain, a small, blond-haired boy of five, coughing out his life while his mother fed hot honey and whiskey to him to stave off the chill.

"There, there," she'd said to him, cradling his head and squeezing his small hands. "No winter's ever been a match for my Willie."

The dream, like a thousand others before it, never lingered as long as he would have wished. Billy wasn't five anymore, wasn't even Willie. No, Willie Delamer, that bright-faced boy, had died at Shiloh, at Gettysburg, in the Wilderness, and at Petersburg. He'd surrendered his name with General Lee at Appomattox Courthouse, lost it again in Abilene and on the Cimarron.

The cold carried him back to Petersburg once more. There, on the darkest night he could ever recall, his friend Travis Cobb had stood on the rampart of the earthen wall of the little fort they'd built.

"Hey, you Yanks!" Trav had called out. "Care for a little contest?"

"What you got in mind, Johnny?" a deep voice boomed from the distant mists.

"Well, we Comanche cavalry over here are about the dandiest singers you ever heard in your entire life."

"You Comanche cavalry don't look to me like you're doin' a lot of cavalryin' these times," the Yank called out.

"Just givin' ole Sheridan a bit of a rest," Trav explained. "Care to test your boys in a little duel?"

"Singin'?" a dozen Yanks asked.

And so Travis Cobb, little more than a skeleton, half a year older though not a hair taller than Billy had been, led the last seventy survivors of the regiment, boys from the river thickets of Texas and the rolling farmlands of Virginia, in a boisterous round of "The Bonnie Blue Flag." The Yanks countered with their fiery new battle hymn. Then the graycoats tried "Dixie" and a pair of old Scottish ballads.

The singing spread down the lines like a summer brush-fire, with unit after unit joining in until a battery of Parrotts

57

couldn't have been heard over the tumult. Finally a lone, weary voice from the Yank lines began the saddest ballad Billy'd ever heard, something called "Johnny's Gone for a Soldier", sung in a high Irish tenor that drifted on the wind until it had silenced the whole of the battlefield.

That ballad had said it all. It told of the loneliness and heartache of a young wife left to carry on life while her young husband was off to the fighting. Cradling babies and spinning cloth, she was forever thinking of her Johnny.

"I got a wife back home my own self," one of the Virginians called out when the song was over.

"Me, too," another shouted.

A strangeness had settled in along the line of trenches as bluecoat and graycoat lost their identity in the black of night. It was Jimmy Earl and Henry talking to Eli and Abner. No one knew or much cared who was from where. In that brotherhood of loneliness they were all cut from the same cloth.

If people could all just sit down at the same table and talk, Billy'd thought, there'd never be any war. For an instant peace had raised its head above the bombproofs. But hours later the cannons had resumed their roar.

"Keep yer head down over there, Eli!" a voice might warn.

"Watch out for them Vermonters on your left!" another might answer.

But it lasted less than a week. Maybe Eli and Jimmy Earl had fallen. More likely they'd remembered they were soldiers.

I could have died a dozen times that year, Billy thought. And maybe a hundred after. It might have made some kind of sense then, leading a charge or holding a trench. But now? What had fate saved him for? Surely not to freeze on a rocky mountainside, a stranger to himself and all around him?

Billy could hear Jason sobbing quietly beside him. Why was it Jason seemed so young? Billy'd been only a year older at Petersburg.

War draped a man in years, wearied him with age. Twenty-five became fifty . . . a lifetime.

Billy wiped cold moisture away from around his eyes. How strange it was to feel such pain at the thought of death! Dying, after all, would end the pain, the suffering, the regret.

Billy felt Jason's shivering shoulder against his own. There might have been a time when Billy would have comforted his companion, but he had learned well that pain always flowed from responsibility. And there was really no comfort to be conveyed in life or in death.

Jason mumbled words between sobs, strange phrases that hinted of home, that spoke of a mother now dead, a home in ashes half a continent away. Billy closed his eyes and hoped the old dream, the warmth of a Brazos summer would return. It didn't. Instead Billy floated along through a frozen void, a nether land of phantoms and faceless shadows that resembled no one so much as they did Billy himself, a trembling figure clothed in eerie crystals of white frost.

Billy was broken out of his spell by the sound of something rattling nearby. He cracked open his frozen eyelids and saw the thatch of pine branches being pulled apart. Before him stood a bearlike apparition, its black fur sprinkled with silver snowflakes.

Billy instinctively fought to reach his pistol, but his hands were stiff and rigid. The framework of the shelter was torn further, and now Jason, too, noticed.

"You still alive?" A burly voice spoke in a strange trilling accent. "Eh? Is there life yet to yer bones?"

Billy managed to nod his head and sit up.

"Never mind yer movin' about just yet, son," the intruder said. "What manner o' beast, be ye? Thief? Scalp hunter? Army deserter? Outlaw?"

"We meant . . . to do . . . some . . . mining," Billy stammered.

"More likely robbin' an honest man of his color," the stranger declared, snatching Billy's pistol, then collecting the rifles as well. "But never ye mind. Ben Grant's no man to leave a coyote to freeze, and you may be fit to put a shoulder to an ax if ye thaw. Best I fetch ye boys home. Crowded we'll be this winter. Unless ye go ahead and die."

Billy looked up into the grizzled old face of his savior. There was no trace of compassion, of surprise, of anything in Ben Grant's eyes. The old man in the bearskin coat had found a pair of frozen creatures and had decided to take them to his home.

Billy tried to form words, but none came. The chill of the wind whistling through the open thatch was stealing his breath. He tried to stand, faltered, and then collapsed. A great darkness fell, smothering his thoughts.

So this is death, he thought. But there seemed to be movement, words, noise. Then nothing again as he passed into unconsciousness.

CHAPTER 9

Billy awoke to find himself lying on a straw mattress in a bed made of pine slats. A heavy woolen blanket lay over him. As his eyes cleared enough for him to examine the rest of his surroundings, he discovered that the bed stood in one corner of a sturdy mountain cabin built of rough-hewn pine logs. The walls were covered with animal hides and drying herbs. Over the mantel hung a short Sharps carbine, the type carried by Federal cavalry during the late war. Nearby was a huge broadsword and a set of battered bagpipes.

The place smelled of wet leather mixed with suet and smoke. It was damp, but the hearth fire spread its warmth throughout the single room. A kettle was bubbling over that fire, and Billy thought he detected the aroma of potatoes with maybe a wild turnip thrown in as well.

Where am I? he asked himself. How did I come to be here?

He recalled only the terrible bite of the north wind, the chill that seemed to penetrate every inch of him. He remembered Jason nearby. Glancing quickly around the cabin, he spotted young McNally lying perhaps five feet away on a similar bed.

The bear, Billy thought as the memory of those burly arms tearing through the thatch wall returned. There'd been a voice, some words now lost in the deep recesses of his mind. Billy studied the two figures now moving about the cabin. Both were slight of frame; surely they were incapable of dragging Jason or himself to safety.

Billy sat up, and a fresh-faced boy of twelve or so moved immediately to his side.

"Here, have a bit of broth," the boy said with a thick accent. "Just sip it, mind you. And don't try to talk just now. I'll be back in a bit."

The boy then returned to his place at the fire. With him was another taller figure. Both had long, slightly wild tresses of strawberry-blond hair. But though both were dressed in similar buckskin trousers and heavy sheepskin coats, Billy knew the older one was a female by her smallish hands and the high-pitched tune she sang softly in some foreign tongue.

He watched the girl as he sipped the broth. She had a kind of grace to her movements, as if each step was well considered and thoughtfully executed. She tended the kettle with rare devotion, stirring it constantly and sprinkling salt or a pinch of herb as the need arose. She appeared totally out of place here in the high country where women were usually large and heavy-boned or else thick-faced Ute or Arapaho.

"Can I bring you more?" the boy asked when Billy had emptied the small bowl of broth. "You'll find your strength soon enough once you've been fed."

"Thanks, but this was enough," Billy said, sitting up and leaning against the wall. "How—"

"Never you mind so much the how. The question more apt to be asked is who. For myself, I'm James Stuart Grant, of the Grants of Glenmoriston. Yon is my sister, Heather."

"I'm called Billy, Billy Cook."

"So, Billy Cook, what manner of foolishness brought you so high on the eve of winter?"

Billy smiled at the boy's high manners, then sighed. How could you explain something you didn't fully understand yourself?

"Eh?" the boy asked.

"Don't know, to be truthful," Billy said. "Young Jason there and I, we were down in Trinidad. We had a little trouble. I got myself shot and robbed. We got those that did it, but we didn't exactly endear ourselves to the town. So I thought, why not follow the Purgatory into the peaks? Who knows? Maybe there's gold in the riverbed like up at Cripple Creek. At worst we ought to find solitude up there."

"Aye, there's plenty of that."

"The storm caught us unprepared. Once I could read the clouds, but lately. . . I don't know. I seem to have lost my feel for the land."

"You had with you an oft-used pistol."

"Yes," Billy said, frowning. "Much too used."

"By you?"

"Yes," Billy admitted, suddenly realizing he hadn't seen his gunbelt, his boots, or even his trousers, for that matter.

"It's put in a safe enough place," James explained.

"It's only prudent to give strangers a wary eye," Billy said, glancing around the room again. Except for the Sharps, there wasn't a hint of gun in the whole cabin.

"We've had bandits down upon us before," the girl spoke from the fireplace. "One nigh shot Jamie no more than a week past."

"Jamie?" Billy mumbled.

"Aye, that's what I'm mainly called," the boy said, sitting on the corner of the bed. "It's common among Scots."

And others, Billy thought, picturing his brother.

"But surely the two of you aren't up in this high country alone?" Billy asked. "You're young to winter in the snows, and besides, I remember something . . . a big man, thick-shouldered, more bear than human."

63

"Papa," Jamie said, smiling. "He's out on the mountain."

"In the snow?"

"Aye, he's accustomed to it. The wind's tame enough now, and there are traps to check, stock to tend."

"Our horses," Billy said, trembling. "Oh, Lord, our horses must be near frozen. There was no shelter for them and—"

"They've been tended," Jamie said, smiling proudly. "I brought them down myself, put them in the stable with Papa's mules. They've had their food, and I rubbed out the cold from their shoulders."

"I owe you for that, Jamie," Billy said, relaxing slightly. "I wouldn't leave a horse to suffer if I could help it."

"Nor Papa, either. He kept an inn on the road to Santa Fe when I was born, and he's had a fine eye for horses and mules ever after. Once I was walking, he had me tending burros and easing the lameness of the pack mules."

"My father taught me to work stock, too."

"Jamie doesn't only tend the mules, mister." Heather spoke up. "He's mule himself, if you were to judge by the smell. You'll forgive us that, I'm hoping, as the Grants as a clan are generally known to be well-washed."

Billy watched young Jamie's face take on the tint of his hair as he gazed at his sister.

"Any fool knows it's unhealthy to bathe when there's a chill to the air," the boy said.

"And in midsummer?" Heather asked. "I've been in sheep pens with less flavor to them than your blankets, Jamie Grant!"

Billy laughed as the two Scots engaged in a heated argument. It took him back to another lifetime, when his own sister had pushed him toward violent action over such trifles as bathing or cutting his hair, wearing shoes or keeping his corner of the cabin neat.

"You'd think she was fifty and my mother!" Jamie exclaimed to Billy. "She's naught but seventeen herself, a mere splinter of a girl. And me, nigh a man, old as Angus Grant was at Culloden Moor."

"A man, he says!" Heather gasped. "Twelve's all, and nae able to wash himself as any civilized man would do."

"I'll wash myself," Jamie said, standing. "When the sun's a bit higher."

"Come spring, perhaps?" Heather asked.

Billy laughed, then began massaging the stiff muscles of his arms and shoulders.

"The soreness will be with you a while," Jamie said, turning away from his sister. "You were nigh frozen when Papa brought you in. You lay like death for three days."

"Three days?" Billy gasped.

"We put you by the fire, then wrapped you in blankets. Heather said sure you were dead, but I knew you'd wake."

"And Jason?" Billy asked, pointing to his companion.

"Aye, he's been up and about some, from the first day on. Heather gives him a nip of spirits, and he sleeps like a babe. Your brother, is he?"

"No," Billy said. "A friend."

"Papa brought him back first, for he was fevered, and I thought him sure to die. But I never fretted over you."

"Oh?"

"Nay, I saw the bullet scars," Jamie said, easing the blanket away from the thin red marks on Billy's shoulder and the other, newer ones on his chest and leg. "I could tell you've known trouble before."

"Yes," Billy said, nodding.

"So Papa turned you over to Heather, and I brought in the horses," Jamie explained. "But we hid your guns. We've known outlaws to come here, though few in winter."

"You took a chance. We might have been thieves."

"Nae such a chance. Heather has a shotgun handy."

The girl pointed to the side of the fireplace, and Billy understood. The gun was ready, should the need arise.

"But it seems a lot of trouble to bring two strangers to your cabin," Billy said. "Winter's always hard, even when you don't add mouths to feed."

"Aye, but there's the work to think of."

"Work?"

"Papa will talk of it later. Your hands are rough, though. You don't dread a day's labor, do you?"

"Never have," Billy said, scratching his beard. "And I've known my share of long days."

"You fought in the war, too," Jamie said, pulling the wrinkled gray hat from beneath the bed. "Cavalry?"

"In Virginia mostly," Billy told the boy. "Tennessee before that."

"We Grants know of lost wars," Heather said, coming to stand beside her brother. "When the Stuart cause died at Culloden, Papa's great-grandfather was transported to Georgia. He worked as a slave for years. From that time, we've never known a home. Until now."

"This mountain's our home, now," Jamie said.

"The Ute once roamed here," Billy said, sighing. "They thought it would be forever, but they were forced off. The Cheyenne say it best. Nothing lasts long, only the earth and sky. There will always be those who rob what should by right belong to you forever, your home, even your name."

Billy stared bitterly at the fire, remembering.

"Up here we're safe," Jamie said, touching Billy's shoulder and speaking with a confidence beyond his years. "All of us."

Billy smiled. It was a great gift, sharing one's sanctuary with a stranger. He hoped it wouldn't prove a mistake, for he remembered how often the dark cloud of violence had followed him.

Suddenly the latch rose, and the door popped open. In walked the short, broad-shouldered man in the bearskin coat that Billy remembered from the evening of the blizzard.

"So, ye've awakened," the man said as Heather helped him out of his coat. "Thought ye might sleep for eternity."

"I'm Billy Cook," Billy said from his bed. "That's Jason McNally over there," he added, pointing to his slumbering companion. "I'm grateful to you for rescuing us from the snow."

"Ben Grant," the grizzled Scotsman said. "It's rare I bring one in from a storm that's still alive. We had a Ute woman with us last winter, though, and Heather learned the healing art from her. A bit of bark or a root cutting, and she brings back the color to a man's face, makes his teeth sound, or casts off the cough."

"I've got some money. I'd pay you for your trouble."

"There's time for such dealings later," old Ben said, collapsing into a wooden chair. "I didn't pull ye from that snowdrift for silver. Nay, there's things a man does."

"And one of them is pay for his keep," Billy said. "I'll be up tomorrow. Surely you can use wood cut or traps set. I'm a fair shot with a rifle if there's game about."

"Not so much now the snow's come," Jamie said. "Deer sometimes."

"Were you able to save the meat we'd packed?" Billy asked.

"Wolves got to it before us," Ben said sadly.

"But you brought in the horses."

"And more," Ben said, producing one of the tin pans bought at the store in Trinidad. "Done much panning?"

"Once," Billy said, noticing the suspicious eyes of the old man. "In the Bighorn country. I thought there might be a trace of color up here, too."

"Aye? What made ye think that?"

"They've found gold in the slopes of the Rockies before. The Purgatory's a swift stream. If there's a vein, the river's bound to have its traces."

"So, yer intent's to mine?"

"And I gather so is yours," Billy said. "I've never moved in on another man's claim, and I won't start now. But I'm able to work. I can help you pan the river this winter. If you say move on come the spring thaw, then it's move on and never a word to anyone. But one man, even with a boy and a near-grown daughter, can't cover the whole length of the river."

"Speak clearly," Ben said.

"We could bind ourselves to a partnership of sorts, the three of you, Jason, and me. A fifth each."

"Heather'd not work the river so much as we would, nor Jamie, either."

"She'll cook then. It's still fair. You're supplying the cabin, most of the gear and provisions. Besides, you know the best places to pan. You've been here. And if trouble comes, it's better to have friends."

"Ye're not posted?" Ben asked.

"No, are you?" Billy said. "If you've panned before, you know what trouble I'm talking about. Renegades, bushwhackers."

"Ye've run across a few in your years, I noticed."

"Yes," Billy admitted. "I know what to do with them. I'm a good shot, and young Jason's learning. We'll protect what's ours, or what's partly ours. When I take a man as a partner, his cares are my cares. His troubles are mine, too."

"Sounds to me like he must be a Scot, Papa," Jamie said, laughing.

"Mostly French," Billy said. "But where I come from, a man's word is better than gold. It's all he is. Without honor, he's nothing."

"Men like that are scarce as beaver," Ben said, stepping toward Billy and extending a hand. "To find two of them in one cabin's a rare stroke of fortune."

Billy gripped the old miner's hand, and the bargain was sealed. And after enjoying a rich beef stew and a pair of old Highland ballads played on Ben's ancient pipes, Billy went back to bed feeling more at home and at peace than he had in ten years.

CHAPTER 10

It was two days before Billy was strong enough to leave the slat bed and venture out onto the mountainside. He envied Jason's rapid recovery.

The privilege of youth, Billy told himself.

Equally amazing was the way Jason made himself a part of the Grant family. One moment he'd be wrestling with Jamie. Then off he'd go to help Heather with her chores. Those dark days on the Cimarron appeared a world away, forgotten along with the gunfire in the lobby of the hotel in Trinidad.

Maybe forgetting is easier when you're young, too, Billy thought. It had never worked for him that way, not at sixteen or at eighteen; not now at twenty-five. The memories were never far distant, and life had taught its lessons well. Don't make friends too easily. Don't open your heart. Pain always follows, creeping in like a winter's chill to steal the gladness, the warmth.

But as the weeks passed, it became impossible for him to keep his distance. The cabin was too small, perhaps. Or maybe it was the snow. It began the first night he joined in the singing of Ben's old ballads. Next Billy helped young Jamie mend a tear in his boot. Soon Billy found himself teaching Heather the Cheyenne way with roots and herbs, showing her which could bring out the taste of dried venison and which could ward off a winter fever.

By mid-December Billy realized he was sharing more than the warmth of the cabin and the kettle of stew. Each time he split wood for the fire or helped Ben reset the traps by the river, Billy grew a little less independent. He worried when Jason and Jamie set off alone into the pines. He cared when Heather cut her finger or when Ben took a tumble down the hillside.

It's too late, he thought as he stared at the blanket of white that covered the land as far as the eye could see. It was worse than wintering with a Cheyenne woman or leading a regiment to battle. Just as he'd adopted Jason's trouble as his own, he'd now taken the Grants to heart, for better or worse, as the Methodist circuit rider used to say when he performed his monthly weddings back on the Brazos. There was no undoing it, no pulling away. Billy was no longer alone.

"We've been awful lucky," Jason said as they sat together beside the fire. "We could've frozen out there, or else run across wolves or grizzlies. Might've been outlaws, too. Instead we found the best people I've ever known."

"You come by luck now and then in this life," Billy said, nodding.

"You know, Ben says he'll teach me the minin' trade come the first thaw. More'n just pannin' for gold, Billy. How to find the vein and dig a tunnel, sink a shaft into the mountain."

"He seems the man to do it."

"And how 'bout that Heather? Isn't she just about the prettiest girl you ever saw?"

Billy turned to look at her. She was busy mending a pair of Jamie's trousers. Even so, her eyes sparkled like stars in the dim light.

"Yes, she's a prize," Billy agreed.

"Suppose I ought to tell her so?" Jason asked.

"Don't know that it'd be news to her," Billy said, laughing. "But I don't suppose a girl can ever be told too many times how pretty she is."

Billy couldn't help smiling when Jason walked to her side and whispered the compliment. Both of them turned a bit pink, and Billy remembered how he'd close to fallen in the river the first time he tried to tell Ellen Cobb how bright her eyes were.

It was strange how much Heather put him in mind of Ellie, how they both moved in the same gentle, easy way. Their faces were so fresh and alive, their touch so soft.

We should have had our years together, Ellie, Billy said silently to a bright December moon, the same moon that bathed the Brazos in its light; the very light that likely sprinkled moonbeams on Ellen somewhere far away. Billy tried not to think of her, lost to him now in a world beyond his touch. He grew cold knowing so many of his youthful dreams were now long dead.

As always, when the recollections weighed heaviest on his mind, Billy turned his attention to work. First he felled two spruces. Then he and Jason sawed the tall trees into foot-and-a-half lengths for the fireplace. Next Billy explored the mountainside, sometimes taking Jamie along. Mostly, though, he walked by himself, hiking across the rock-strewn land, trying to escape memories of other winters in other places.

Each time he returned to the cabin, shivering from the biting December wind and feeling stiff from old wounds.

"It's an old man's curse, Billy," Ben told him. "Winter in the Rockies seems to find every wee bend in a man's bones. If ye've taken it into yer head to go prancing across the country, maybe I can persuade ye to shoulder yer rifle and see if there's any game to be found. I wouldn't turn away a venison steak or a turkey leg just now."

"We'll go tomorrow," Jason said. "Billy and I, we're a fair team when it comes to huntin'."

"Well, now, actually I had in mind to use ye down on the river, Jason my boy," Ben said. "Billy will be needing a bit of help bringing in any game he might shoot, though. Maybe there's someone else who could go."

Jamie needed no further hint. In an instant he shot across the room, clamped a firm if small hand on Billy's shoulder, and pleaded to go.

"I've shot rabbits with the Sharps," the boy said.

"Couldn't've been a lot of rabbit left," Billy said, staring at the big gun.

"He's welcome to take my Winchester," Jason said.

"Papa?" Jamie asked.

"It's time he learned to stalk a deer," Ben said. "Up to now, we haven't done much hunting in the winter, getting by on fish and what finds its way into our traps. It'd be a service if ye'd take him along, Billy."

"I know the mountains," Jamie pointed out.

Billy thought about it. It didn't take two to hunt, and Jamie would be of more use at the cabin. But with the boy along, there'd be less chance of freezing to death or becoming lost.

"Then it's agreed?" Heather asked. "I expect you two to bring back something good for my kettle."

"We will," Jamie promised.

Billy was less certain. In winter, game was scarce, even in the lowlands. The high country was left to the eagles and owls, or perhaps to the ghosts of long-dead Ute and Cheyenne. Even the grizzlies passed the cold months hibernating in caves. But the thought of fresh meat spurred him on.

Billy and his young companion bundled themselves in every scrap of wool that could be located. Billy borrowed a heavy coat of buffalo hide from old Ben, as well as a beaver hat.

"Do we have to wear all these clothes?" Jamie complained. "I don't think I'll be able to walk, much less fire a gun."

"You'll be glad enough of the wool when the wind sweeps over the mountain cutting through you like a knife," Billy told him.

"I've grown up here," Jamie said, picking up Jason's

Winchester and pointing it toward the door. "I know about the wind and the cold."

"Then you know we're apt to be out in it a while."

"Maybe we'll be lucky. I saw a doe just yesterday."

"Where?"

"Just past the east trap line. I'll show you."

Billy slipped on a pair of gloves, took his rifle, and followed the boy outside. Once past the door, he winced. The harsh north wind swept whirls of snow into his eyes, and he moved sideways to blunt its effect.

"It's this way," Jamie called, trudging through the snowdrifts as if wading through a summer stream. The boy wove his way through the tall pines and rugged boulders, nimbly climbing the icy ledges above the river, always urging Billy on.

It's like the Shoshoni say, Billy thought. Some are born to the mountains. They become one with the trees and the rocks. It was how he'd been back on the Brazos, swimming its waters, riding its valleys, knowing every inch of the land like an old friend.

If, as the Cheyenne believed, there was a spirit to a place, that spirit would gladly give of itself to a boy like Jamie; would bring the sought-after deer to lend its strength to a boy's twelfth winter. Billy'd seen it a hundred times, how nature gave of itself to foster life, how the buffalo gave its life to feed the hungry and to clothe the bare.

The Indians know, Billy thought as he struggled against the deep snow and the cold to keep up with Jamie. Hunting was done with a reverence, a respect for the prey. Always before hunting the buffalo, prayers were made. A man shot from need, reluctantly, not with the boastful shouts of a hide hunter.

What was it old Yellow Shirt had said? A man shouldn't stray from the circle of life. He had to maintain his ties with the world. Billy wondered if that was what had gone wrong. Had he left that circle, walked too long in a world of strange men who knew nothing of life, who dealt death as they would cards to a gambler?

"You all right, Billy?" Jamie called from the rocks ahead.

"Yes," Billy answered.

"The leg bothering you? I shouldn't go so fast."

"The leg's near mended," Billy said, touching the wound, now knitted over and no longer bleeding.

"I'm sorry," Jamie said, grasping Billy's left elbow and leading the way onward. "I get up here and I forget everything. There's such a freedom about the mountains, especially in winter. You'd swear there wasn't another person alive in the whole world."

"I know," Billy said, nodding. "I passed a winter in the Bighorns back in '67. We hunted elk, mountain goats, some big sheep."

"We?"

"I had a partner. And for a time we had a pair of Shoshoni with us. Then the army came along to guard the Bozeman Road, and Red Cloud moved his Sioux up along the Powder River. The Shoshoni went back home."

"And you?"

"Stayed awhile, mostly in the mountains up north where the Crow live. Then I headed south."

"I saw your pistol. Have you shot a lot of men with it?"

"Some," Billy said, sighing. "Too many. I was in the war, Jamie. I suppose I got used to the killing, what with hundreds, sometimes thousands falling all around me. Then, when it was supposed to be over, I tried to go home. But the killing didn't stop. At first I felt like it was a duty, standing up for what was right. But I guess it's more a matter of what side you're on, just like the war. What's right to you's often wrong to the other man. It comes down to who's fastest."

"And that was you."

Billy didn't answer, just stared off down the valley. Jamie's grip grew firmer, and they continued on toward the trap line.

"Papa isn't much for hunting," Jamie said, inspecting the first of the traps. "He's a good trapper. He learned the beaver trade from his father. And we fish."

"My father took me hunting for rabbits the first summer I could carry a rifle. Sometimes we went with the Indians after deer. I once hunted buffalo with Comanches down in Texas. My father ran cattle as a cash crop, and we depended on game for food."

"I once saw some buffalo hunters. They shot a whole herd, close to fifty, I guess. For hides, Papa said."

"And left the meat to rot on the plains," Billy said, kicking snow into the air. "I've seen Cheyenne near starved, the little ones swelled up, their eyes empty with hunger. There's scarcely a herd left along the Republican. God provided everything a man needs on this earth, food and medicine, if he knows how to make use of it. But some men only know the killing way, and a starving time's sure to follow."

"Will you teach me to hunt the way you taught Heather about the roots and such?"

"If there's time," Billy said.

"There will be. We've got the rest of the winter before you could leave, even if you wanted to. And you might choose to stay."

"I might," Billy said, studying the deepening woods. "But lately whenever I think I've found a place to stay, someone comes along to change it."

"No one's coming up here," Jamie said, laughing.

"Jason and I did. Sooner or later others will, too. There's no place left for a man to find solitude, especially if there's gold to be taken from a river."

"Papa worries about that, too."

"He should," Bill said soberly. "Pueblo's full of renegades, and Denver's awash with thieves. It's not the best of times to be alone with a girl and a boy."

"We're not alone, though," Jamie said, releasing Billy's arm and starting through the pines. "You're here."

Jamie's blue eyes filled with brightness as he spoke, and Billy tried not to notice. He'd opened his heart too often, only to feel the sharp sting of disappointment and loss. But a man can choke on loneliness.

"I have a younger brother named Jamie," Billy said as he followed. "I used to take him hunting."

"After deer?"

"Spring and fall. He wasn't much of a shot, though. He had Mama's love for books and poetry."

"What became of him?"

"He reads law down in Texas. So I've heard. I don't keep in touch with my family."

"And you never married?"

"No. There was a girl once, but . . . well, we went our separate ways."

"Heather's taken with you," Jamie said, laughing in that way younger brothers have when judging the foolishness of older sisters. "She's a good cook, and there's plenty of room here for a second cabin."

"Don't you think she's a bit young for me?"

"Mama was a full twelve years younger than Papa. Heather's not so bad to look at, Billy, and—"

"And?" Billy asked, interrupting.

"Well, you'd have me around, like a brother, you see."

"Think I need another brother, do you?" Billy asked, reaching out and holding the boy firmly by the shoulder.

"Somebody's got to keep you from freezing to death in a blizzard next winter."

Billy couldn't help smiling at the boy. There was a trace of something in Jamie's eyes, a half-forgotten mischief Billy'd once possessed himself.

He's too much like I was, Billy decided. A boy like that, well, he was clearly doomed to be disappointed in life. But for the moment Jamie's youthful stride and boyish optimism carried them both into the heart of the pines, searching out the small tracks of a doe in the hardening snow.

"Tracks are fresh," Billy whispered.

Jamie stepped aside and Billy took the lead. The two became as one, more shadow than hunter, slipping around the tall pines until they were upwind of the trail. Then, near a small frozen pond, Billy saw the deer.

"Which one?" Jamie asked, cradling the Winchester.

76

"The tallest of the bucks, there," Billy whispered as the wind stung his face. "Your shot, little brother."

Jamie gazed upward for a second, smiling, then took his aim. The boy held the rifle steadily, and Billy sensed that Jamie'd shot before, and perhaps often. The rifle sang out, ripping the snow from nearby branches. The buck stepped back, its shoulder torn by the shot. But as the other deer scattered, the buck staggered after them.

Billy never hesitated. He leveled his own rifle, fixed the wounded animal in his sights, and fired. The buck's head snapped back, and then it fell, lifeless, into the snow.

"Good shot," Jamie said, slapping Billy's back. "I thought we might have to follow it. Papa and I once chased a doe better than two miles."

"I didn't think you'd been hunting often," Billy said, standing.

"Well, Papa thought you might need a little time away from the cabin."

"He was right," Billy said as he headed toward the buck.

"He usually is," Jamie shouted, plunging through the snow after Billy.

It's a comfort, having a father who is right about life, Billy thought as he drew out his knife to make the throat cut.

"Fresh meat's going to be welcome," Jamie said. "Maybe we'll come back and find ourselves a turkey for Christmas."

Christmas, Billy thought, remembering the winter feasts of his childhood, the warmth of a fire, and the love that flooded the cabin. It had been almost ten years since Billy'd celebrated the holiday.

"We'll do that, Jamie," Billy said as he prepared to butcher the buck.

"Be sure to save the hide. It'll make a good pair of trousers, maybe a shirt."

"Maybe both if the body's not too big," Billy said, wondering how long it'd take to work the hide and do the sewing. Jamie's face glowed, and Billy felt that mixture of

77

warmth and fear that always came with opening his heart. But he supposed no matter how many times a man bled from disappointment, he'd continue to gamble on the notion that someday he would discover that peace, that sought-after refuge from the pain and sorrow that too often visited life.

Purgatory, he thought as they carried the travois with the meat back to the cabin. Certainly it was more than the name of a river. It was the nature of life. And maybe he had, at last, found the key to the higher, brighter path he'd hunted for so long.

CHAPTER 11

The bitterly cold days of mid-December arrived, painting the rocky mountainside in layers of silvery white snow. The tall pines and spruces seemed draped in ivory shawls of the soft powder. Under the bright midday sun, the frozen Purgatory River sparkled, and the surrounding ridges glimmered. At night a northerly wind moaned across a forlorn land.

Aside from the thin swirl of smoke rising from the chimney of old Ben Grant's cabin, there wasn't a sign of life. Even the beavers and eagles had abandoned the high country. Twice each week Billy set off into the woods in search of deer, usually accompanied by Jason McNally or young Jamie Grant. Sometimes the hunters would return with fresh meat. But game was scarcer than ever, and more and more Billy led the way back to the cabin with nothing to show for the hours spent fighting the cruel, cold north wind.

"I thought I knew what it was like to be cold," Jason remarked as they returned to the cabin one afternoon.

"Not like the plains in summer, is it?" Billy asked, peeling off his wet coat.

"I remember snow back east, but nothing like this," Jason said, putting the rifles away. "I feel like I'll never be warm again."

"You will," Billy said, holding his hands over the fire. "I've been cold before and I've been hot before. Time'll come when it's worse. January in the Rockies is bitter cold. February's even colder. March can be bad, too."

"Had snow in April last year," Ben added.

"You sure findin' gold's worth all this?" Jason asked Billy.

"Gold?" Billy asked, scratching his head. "Wasn't gold I came for."

"Then what?" Heather asked, joining them.

"What?" Jamie echoed.

They gathered around Billy, and he tried to avoid their probing eyes. The question wouldn't go away, though, and he finally spoke.

"I'm not altogether sure," he told them. "Solitude, maybe. A fresh start."

"Many's the man who took to the high country hoping to find something more in himself than he saw in the lowlands," Ben said. "But I suspect what's there always was."

"Sometimes a man wants to be something better," Billy said, his eyes flashing with intensity. "Only down there, in the towns, with people all around, he doesn't always have a chance. He needs some distance . . . some miles between himself and his troubles."

"Sure," Jason agreed.

"He can't run from himself," Ben said to both of them. "Can't hide, either. Towns have their way of following a man."

And so does the trouble, Billy thought.

But as the rest of December rolled by, he couldn't imagine a better place to be. Yes, it was cold, but there were plenty of pine logs for the fire and more than enough food for his belly. The sturdy cabin kept out the biting wind, and the soft voice of Heather and the admiring eyes of Jamie fended off the loneliness.

When not roaming the icy mountainside in search of deer, Billy occupied himself with working the rough hides into soft buckskin. Although none of them kept a regular calendar, Christmas was not far off, and there were gifts to prepare. Tanning hides in freezing weather wasn't the easiest task, but Billy remembered how the Shoshoni worked the skins back and forth against a stone, even chewed them sometimes. He couldn't hide his delight when the buckskins grew supple, pliable. It was then time to shape them into their final form: a small shirt for Jamie, a larger one for Heather. Vests were managed for Jason and Ben.

The sewing was difficult. Billy managed to snatch a needle from Heather's sewing box, but for thread all he had was a kind of brittle thread he made from deer sinew. Never known for his talents as a tailor, Billy feared he would never fix the sleeves on the shirts without pricking himself to death.

He had just managed to complete the gifts when Ben finally announced that it must surely be Christmas. The day of the celebration was chosen less because the stars were right or the days had been counted than because the woodpile stood high and all work was done.

"The Lord understands a man must attend to his labors," Ben was fond of saying, and Christmas must fit itself between tasks. No sooner had Heather lit candles and Jason brought in a small pine than snow began falling outside, a gentle, dreamlike sprinkling that was perfect for the occasion.

"Ye see?" Ben asked the others. "Now have ye ever seen such a snow? It must be we've chosen the proper day."

Watching the snowfall, Billy couldn't argue the point. For once the wind eased. Jason shot a beautiful turkey, and when the bird was plucked, Heather had it dressed and baking in a dutch oven.

"Have ye ever witnessed a feast such as this?" Ben asked when they sat down that evening to roast turkey and boiled potatoes, complemented with the last of the peas put by that summer. Two tins of peaches were opened as well. To top off the dinner, Ben produced an ancient bottle of Kentucky whiskey, and even Jamie was allowed a swallow or two.

"For old times and old friends not with us," Ben cried out, raising his glass.

"And to new friends and better days," Jason added, touching his glass to Ben's.

Billy added his own glass to the others and drank to both toasts. As the liquor burned its way down his throat, he thought sadly of the many old friends who were, indeed, absent. But he couldn't help smiling as he glanced at the warmth in the eyes of his companions, the new family he'd found in the midst of deepest winter.

Other toasts followed, pledges to each other and wishes for success once the river thawed. Dreams of great sacks full of gold mixed with visions of a bright and shining spring. And all the while Billy's eyes drank in the wonder of a family that had somehow withstood hardship and found an occasion to laugh and to enjoy even a frozen wasteland like the Spanish Peaks in December.

When the last of the food and drink was devoured, Billy helped Heather clear the table of platters and bowls, pewter forks and knives. Ben and Jamie disappeared for a time, only to reappear in broad bolts of plaid, marching with knees high in the air as Ben played his tired old bagpipes.

Billy couldn't help laughing in spite of the serious glance sent his way by Ben. There'd been a regiment of New York Highlanders in Virginia, so it wasn't that Billy'd never seen a man in a kilt before. It was the high stepping and bold, military tempo of the music that brought a smile to his face.

"Have ye n'er seen a true Grant before?" Ben demanded when the notes died away. "My grandfather marched in this plaid, and his before him!"

"Must be English blood in him somewhere," Jamie suggested, fighting to keep a solemn face.

"Aye, or Hanover German," Ben added, wiping his forehead and beginning a fresh tune on the pipes.

Billy sat on the edge of the hearth and watched as Heather appeared, decked out in a plaid dress with matching sash and bonnet. She joined her brother in a wild, freewheeling dance. Knees kicking high in the air, the two Grants linked elbows and swung each other around the room.

Jason retreated to Billy's side, staring in disbelief at the dancers.

"Well, what's keeping ye two so idle?" Ben called out once the dance was over.

"I've still got a game leg," Billy said, rubbing the scar on his thigh. "Besides, I never was much of a dancer, even when I knew the steps."

"Nor me," Jason said, shaking his head.

But Heather reached out and pulled them to her, and the music resumed. Billy started with the girl, then found himself locking elbows with first Jamie, then Jason.

This is pure craziness, Billy thought, feeling his leg burn with each attempted kick. But in truth it was fun, and the four of them stomped around the cabin, jumping and kicking and doing their best to keep in step with Ben's piping. For a time Jamie attempted to play the pipes, but it was mostly a failure, and Ben took over again, complaining that boys born lately had no knack for music.

"Well, I do for dancing," Jamie boasted, and he and Heather spread out the old broadsword, then rested a musket across it to form an X. Then they performed a Highland fling that satisfied even their father's critical eye.

"Now it's your turn," Jamie said, pulling Billy to his feet and dragging him to Heather.

"Here now," she said, folding Billy's arms and placing Jamie's bonnet on Billy's head. "Just watch how I step between the blades and do the same."

Billy would have run if there'd been any possible escape, but the snow outside was heavy, and the cabin had but one room.

"Come on, Billy," Jason said, laughing. "Just do the same as Heather."

"I could watch her till spring and still make a fool of myself," Billy answered, stepping back. But Jason and Jamie pushed him toward her again, and Ben began piping.

Oh, Lord, help me, Billy thought as he did his best to mirror Heather's graceful steps. But it was like a bull moose trying to match strides with a white-tailed doe. Or a prairie hen trying to fly after an eagle. Finally Billy tripped over the sword and rolled into a heap on the floor. The cabin filled with laughter, and even Billy had to smile in spite of his throbbing leg.

"He'll never make a proper Highlander," Ben announced.

"Perhaps he'd do better with a kilt," Jamie suggested.

"I believe I've been venturesome enough for today," Billy said, dragging himself to one corner. "I prefer trousers, if it's all the same."

"Must be English," Ben grumbled. "Cook? Sure, he's likely from Liverpool or some such."

The cabin filled with laughter again, and the dancing was left to Heather, Jamie, and a reluctant Jason McNally.

"The Irish take a turn at the pipes, lad," Ben claimed. "You'll be a fine dancer, I'm sure."

But Jason lasted only half as long as Billy, and the broadsword and rifle were restored to their places on the wall. Ben continued piping, but now Heather led the singing of a trio of old Scottish ballads, the last sadder than any Billy'd heard before.

"It's an old, old tune," she explained, "all about a girl mourning for her love. He's gone off to fight with the Bruce against the English, and she knows he'll not return."

"Yes, that's the way with war and sweethearts," Billy said, his eyes growing moist.

"Enough of such mournful talk!" Ben shouted, breaking the spell of gloom. "We've celebrating to do. Jamie, my boy, fetch the bag!"

Jamie flew across the room and dug a large woolen sack

from behind an oak chest. The boy dragged the bag to his father, then sat beside old Ben.

"It's customary to share our bounty this time of year," Ben explained as he reached inside the bag. "We've no stores or freight depots nearby, so you'll excuse the gift for its smallness."

Ben then presented small bundles to each of them. For Heather there were new sewing needles and a yellow dress kept back from a trip to Pueblo months before. Jamie received a Sharps carbine purchased from a trapper. Ben's children presented him with a pipe and tobacco. Ben handed Jason a heavy coat made of buffalo hide.

"For you," Ben said, looking at Billy, "we found a bit of the plaid."

Billy accepted several yards of fabric from Heather.

"I thought to make you a kilt," she said, "but Jamie said you might not care so much for bare legs, being once from Texas."

"A shirt would do nicely," Billy said, smiling as Jamie laughed.

"My gift to you stands in the oven," Heather announced. "A pie."

"We'll have it afterward," Ben said, passing the now empty sack to Heather.

"I've gifts as well," Jamie said, rushing to his bed for a minute, then returning with small blocks of wood carved in the shapes of animals. For Ben there was a grizzly bear. Heather accepted a deer. Jamie handed Jason a wolf, then gave Billy what surely was the best of all, a hawk in full flight.

"I suppose it's my turn now," Billy said, stepping to his blankets and producing the carefully concealed gifts. "For you, Ben," he said, handing over the first vest. "And Jason," he added, passing the other one to young McNally.

"And what about me?" Jamie asked.

"Well, first I've got something for your sister," Billy told the boy as he presented Heather with a shirt and a pair of moccasins.

"And all this from deer I trailed," Jamie grumbled.

"Then I suppose it's proper you should get something," Billy admitted, tossing Jamie the best of the shirts, big enough to allow a summer's growth and decorated with bold eagles in the Cheyenne fashion. "Although I know you Scots fail to appreciate the touch of buckskin against your knees, I made trousers as well."

Jamie took the last of the clothes and clutched Billy's arm. Billy tried to step away, but the boy held on tightly until Billy surrendered. He touched the boy's reddish hair lightly, remembering another boy left behind long ago.

"Thank you, Billy," Heather said, resting her head against his chest.

"No, it's me that's in your debt," Billy said, pulling her tightly against him. "First for my life. Then for the warmth of your cabin. And finally for sharing—sharing . . ."

"We know, lad," Ben said, a hint of a tear in his weary eye. "It's the season for family."

Yes, Billy thought as Jason surprised them by producing gifts as well, fishing poles for Ben and Jamie, carved wooden ladles and spoons for Heather, a fine new razor for Billy.

"That could be put to good use," Heather said, scratching Billy's beard.

"It belonged to Loman," Jason whispered. "I hope that doesn't mean it will bring ill fortune."

"A blade's a blade," Billy said, clasping his friend's hand. "Though I'm afraid we'll soon need another one."

Jason touched his sparse whiskers and smiled, but it was Jamie who spoke.

"Highland folk prefer to let their beards grow," the boy said, stroking invisible whiskers.

They all laughed, and Ben took up the pipes again. They sang for half the night, pausing only to eat Heather's pie and to read from an old yellowing Bible. Finally, when the last ounce of energy was spent, they crept to their beds.

Billy lay in his blankets, staring through the small crack in the window shutter at the bright sky above the mountain. The snow had stopped, and the stars overhead danced in the ebony blackness of the night.

Another year's soon laid to rest, Billy thought as he watched those stars. Or maybe it's gone already, and this is 1872. Shiloh and its dead are a decade past, and Mama and Papa are a long time buried. Ellen's wed to someone else.

He coughed away a tear and pulled the blankets tight against his chest.

Ellen, do you even remember me? Billy wondered. And he hoped not. It was a heavy burden to bear, this always remembering. Now a new year was coming, with new hopes and a fresh dream. Billy remembered the softness of Heather's hair against his cheek, the fierce grasp of little Jamie's hands. Yes, a new belonging had come.

Lord, let me stay this time, Billy prayed. Let me stay.

CHAPTER 12

Billy hoped the peaceful spell that Christmas had cast across the Spanish Peaks might remain until spring, but there was rarely any real peace to be found at any time. So he wasn't too surprised when the quiet of one winter night was shattered by a thrashing sound outside the cabin. The shrill cries of horses and the bawling of mules brought him to his feet, and as he pulled on his trousers and searched for his coat, he heard a low grunt amid the noise of splintering planks coming from the direction of the animal shed.

Ben sat up warily in his bed, and Jason and Jamie rubbed sleep from their eyes. Only Heather was up, a robe about her shoulders, and it was to her that Billy addressed himself as he loaded the magazine of his Winchester.

"Something's out there," he told her. "Maybe a bear. I'll take a look."

"Alone?" Heather asked, a wrinkle of concern appearing on her forehead.

"Anybody else look like he's ready to go?" Billy asked, pulling on his boots. "Don't worry yourself. I know what to do."

Before Heather could voice an objection, Billy slipped out of the cabin into the paralyzing cold and plowed his way through the deep snowdrifts. As he went, his eyes searched through the powdery mist for some sign of the trouble.

It didn't take long for him to locate the source of the disturbance. Between a tall spruce and the pine planks of the animal shed was an eerie mountain of fur, painted silver-white by frost and snow, hurling its bulk against the walls of the shed.

Can't be a bear, Billy told himself as he swung the lever of the rifle, engaging a round in the firing chamber. Bears sleep through the winter. But as he fixed the creature in his sights, the monster turned, revealing fierce eyes and a mouth full of razorlike teeth.

Billy fired twice in rapid succession, and the bear moved off into the trees, dragging its hind foot and grunting angrily. Billy might have fired a third time, but the cold had numbed his fingers and he could no longer work the lever. At any rate, the bear had vanished into the snowdrifts, leaving the ivory landscape spotted with its blood.

"What was it?" Ben asked when Billy stumbled back inside the cabin. "What'd ye see, lad?"

"I'm not entirely sure," Billy said, securing the door and making his way to the fire. "A bear, I think."

"Bear?" Ben asked, scratching his beard. "Sure it wasn't human?"

"I never saw a man tear through pine planks with his bare hands, and this one had to be a thousand pounds, easy."

"Bears hibernate," Heather said, putting a kettle on the fire.

"This one had a hungry look about him," Billy explained. "Could be he didn't fatten himself enough to last the season. I've seen it before. They wake early, pure angry at the world, ready to strike anything in sight."

"You killed him, though, didn't you?" Jason asked.

"No," Billy said, shaking his head.

"But we heard the shots," Jamie added. "You hit him?"

"Once, maybe twice," Billy told them. "There's blood on the snow. But the cold got to my hands."

"Any animal's dangerous once wounded," Ben said, scratching his beard again. "This one'll be back. Hungry's bad. Hurt's worse. We'd best be on our guard for a time."

"That won't be enough," Billy said, warming as the fire drove the numbness from his knees and toes. "Night's no time to hunt bears. Come morning, it's best I trail him."

"May not be much of a trail with the snow and all," Jason pointed out.

"Thing like that's bound to snap off branches, make a path," Billy said, resting the Winchester against the wall of the cabin and accepting a cup of tea from Heather. "Trust me to do this. I've tracked my share of animals."

"Human and otherwise," Jason said, laughing.

Billy turned away and stared out the window. Out there in the distance was the bear, cold, hurt, hungry—and alone. As always, his heart was with the hunted, the lonely of the world in search of refuge. And like before with the buffalo along the Republican River in Kansas or that band of Comanche raiders back in Palo Pinto County, Billy knew it was his fate to be the hunter, the one destined to bring about their end.

Billy tried to go back to sleep, but each time he closed his eyes, he saw the bear again, its great bulk shaking the walls of the cabin, its huge paws tearing through windows as it fought to strike out at its tormentors.

That's how it is with pain, Billy thought. It makes you hard. You want to scream out into the night, hit out at anyone and anything in sight. You want to make someone else hurt as much as you do. But, in the end, it's pointless. The killing, the maiming—none of it numbs the pain. And the shadow it casts chokes off all that's left of the good a man feels.

By the time the sun rose above the pines and drove off the mountain mists, Billy was bundled in his thickest clothing. The Winchester's magazine was full, and spare shells filled one pocket of Billy's coat.

"I'll be going with ye, lad," Ben announced as they ate their breakfast.

"To what effect?" Billy asked. "You need to mend the stable and see to the needs of the stock. I know what to do. Trust me to see that it's done."

"Then take the lads," Ben said, pointing to Jason and Jamie.

"Better they stay here," Billy said grimly.

"I'm going!" Jamie declared. "I know the land better than you do, and, besides, we hunt together."

"Not this time," Billy declared. "You stay as well, Jason McNally," Billy added, looking at his young friend. "A single man's better on a job like this."

"Is he?" Jason asked. "As I recall, you didn't fare so well the last time you set off by yourself."

Billy nodded. But the remark failed to change his mind and he left the cabin alone.

Trailing the bear was not the easy task he had made it out to be. An early-morning snowfall had obscured the tracks, and the animal had headed toward a rocky side of the hill where there were few trees. Billy had about given up on the trail when he heard a branch snap a few yards behind him.

He turned quickly, fully prepared to discover a thousand pounds of wounded bear approaching. Instead he came face-to-face with Jamie Grant.

"Good Lord!" Billy shouted. "I could've shot you dead. What on earth are you doing here?"

"Somebody had to come and keep you out of trouble," Jamie said, grinning shyly. "Jason and I flipped a coin. I won."

"You're going back," Billy declared.

"I'm staying," Jamie said, stepping forward until his face nearly touched Billy's chest. "I've been watching you. You've lost the trail. I told you. We're partners. And I know where it's headed."

"You what?"

"There are some caves on the other side of this hill,"

Jamie said, pointing with his hand in that direction. "We shot a brown bear there last summer."

"Now that you've told me, you can go back to the cabin."

"You'll never find the way alone."

"I will."

"I'm not tall yet, Billy, but it's been a long time since anybody's needed to look out for me."

"Oh? Is it something you outgrow?"

Jamie seemed surprised at Billy's question. Billy found himself smiling. He had always assumed that fearlessness came with a few extra inches, that courage was something a man acquired with his first whiskers.

"Scared?" Billy asked the boy.

"A little," Jamie admitted. "You?"

"A little," Billy answered, stepping aside so that the boy could lead the way.

The ground proved treacherous, rocky and icy, and Billy slipped more than once. He made sure the firing chamber in his rifle was empty. He'd known men to fall and shoot their legs off hunting in midwinter. Jamie, on the other hand, sprinted up the hillside like a mountain goat, weaving his way through the tall trees as nimbly as a circus acrobat. In a quarter hour they'd left behind the barren hillside and entered a region of craggy rocks and dark, foreboding caves.

"We're here," Jamie whispered.

Billy knew it already. There were traces of blood on broken pine branches, and the whole place smelled of something dead. There were a dozen caves, though, and locating the right one wouldn't be easy. As Billy tried to think of a plan of action, a small spruce toppled to the ground, and an anguished snarl filled the air.

"There, Billy!" Jamie hollered, retreating from the path of the lumbering beast. "There!"

Billy swung the steel lever of the Winchester down and back, advancing the first shell into the firing chamber. Then he fired at the bear. The first shot stunned the beast, knocking it backward. But the animal was beyond pain, past fear. It drew itself up high on its back feet and clumsily surged forward.

"Billy!" Jamie screamed as the bear approached.

For the first time Billy grew nervous. The creature was bleeding badly from its chest and hindquarters. Billy fired again and again, tearing away at the bear's huge body from close range. Still it came on. Billy read death in the animal's glazed eyes, and the bellowing that filled the air around the hillside told of it. But a dying creature can often strike out fiercely in its final moment. Billy fired a fourth time and a fifth, fired until he could feel the barrel of the Winchester growing hot. Finally, as the bear closed the final few feet, he turned to run away. The monster dove onward, though, as if possessed by some hidden strength, some unearthly power.

A paw tore at Billy's leg, opening a gash across his thigh. Billy rolled backward as the bulk of the bear knocked the rifle away. He gazed up in disbelief as he realized he was defenseless.

But the bear had done its worst. The Winchester's bullets had found their mark; the huge furry demon breathed a final time and then collapsed.

"You got it," Jamie announced, rushing to Billy's side. In the boy's trembling fingers was the missing Winchester. "Almost waited too long, though, didn't you?" Jamie said with a gasp.

"Almost," Billy admitted, examining the shallow tears in his pants leg where bright red blood seeped out.

"Here," Jamie said, opening his coat and tearing a strip from his white shirt. "Bind it with this."

Billy nodded, then tied the cloth tightly around the wound.

"Heather's always remarking how fond she is of bear grease," Jamie said, stepping over to the fallen beast. "We'll eat a month on this one."

"Not a month," Billy said, sadly observing how thin the bear appeared to be. It took a great hunger to send a brown bear hunting in the heart of January.

"You'll have yourself a good coat from him."

"Better yet, a rug for the cabin," Billy said. "You think you can help me get to my feet?"

Jamie turned back to Billy and offered his smallish hand in assistance. Billy regained his feet, then flexed his thigh. The bleeding worsened, but it clearly was a minor hurt. The muscles worked as always, and the pain was nothing compared to that which Billy'd known back in the fall.

"Glad I came along now?" Jamie asked, reaching an arm around Billy's waist, taking some of the weight off Billy's injured leg.

"Well, I knew you were a fair partner, Jamie Grant."

"Only fair?" Jamie asked, frowning. "Next time I'll leave you to the bear."

Billy smiled. The killing had returned, but it was gone now, swept away as the wind took away a winter storm. Yes, there'd been death, as there always was in the high country. But in its wake came life—and hope.

In the week that followed the shooting of the bear, Billy watched the wound on his thigh heal so that only the slightest hint of a scar remained. And he hoped that, come spring, the deeper, older wounds would heal as well, and he would find himself the new start he craved more than anything.

CHAPTER 13

Winter spent itself in whirlwind and blizzard, piercing cold and snowdrifts deep enough to swallow a person. Billy passed the rest of January and February tending the animals or scaring up a rare rabbit or deer for the table. And in spite of the frigid temperatures, he was warmed by that rare gift of belonging freely bestowed by the Grants. By the middle of March he'd even become fond of the bagpipes. He'd grown almost passionate about the old ballads Heather sang in her high, sweet voice.

It seemed as if a hundred years had passed since Billy'd belonged anywhere. Now he felt as much a part of the cabin as its stone chimney. Yes, after so many miles he'd finally found a place to rest, to pause, and perhaps to stay.

It was April before the first cracks appeared in the river. Soon sections of ice broke apart and drifted to shore. Ben had them go out each day, cutting squares of the ice to save for summer.

"They'll prove most useful," Ben said as they carried the ice up the hill for storage in what appeared to be a small dugout.

"Keeps meat from spoiling in summer," Jamie explained as they filled the place. "Sometimes if we don't come up with enough skins from the traps or gold from the riverbed, we sell the ice to the townspeople."

It seemed a strange cash crop to Billy, but he'd grown to rely on Ben Grant's judgment. The old Scotsman knew the high country and its ways.

Ben Grant knew the miner's craft as well. Once the thawing ice on the mountains began to fill the river with runoff, sweeping the last remaining frozen patches downstream, Ben had everyone out sifting through the bottom in search of golden flakes.

"Never did I see much in the way of nuggets in a river," Ben told Billy as they worked one afternoon. "But once the color shows herself, it's an easy bit of work to follow her to where the vein's hidden."

"I've hunted gold before myself," Billy said. "Often as not, there is no vein, just a bit of gold sprinkled across a bed of quartz.."

"Aye, but there's a vein in this river, or near enough to be got at," Ben declared. "I've felt it in my bones, this golden heart of the mountains. I've been after it each year. Why, we've dug half the bottom from this river the past three summers. Each year there's fresh color. It's bound to be brought out of these hills, lad. It's here, and that's for certain."

"For certain," young Jamie echoed.

Billy hoped so. All too often he'd seen the shattered hopes of men who bet their fortunes on a distant dream. Failure brought despair, drunkenness, and death in the end.

But each day as he waded into the Purgatory, his trousers rolled up to the thighs, Billy dipped his flat-bottomed tin pan into the sandy bottom, swirled and sifted water and silt in search of the yellow flakes that might bring their dream into reality.

There was easier work a man could do. From before sunrise to dusk, Billy worked his way along the riverbed, sandwiched between Ben and Jason, with Jamie and Heather working the opposite bank. Toes and legs grew numb from the icy water. Knees were torn and bruised from frequent falls caused by the swift-flowing stream. In the evening Billy sat by the fire rubbing his weary shoulders and fighting the pain that crawled up his back.

"Comes with age," Ben told him as Heather rubbed horse liniment into his aching muscles. "Was a time when I could work a stream half into tomorrow. But no more. The sun's my clock now. I rise with her, and I put an end to my labors when she bids good night."

"That's the way it is on a ranch," Jason said. " 'Cept we usually got up when Ma's roosters took to crowin'. Half the time there'd be a harness to mend or night guard to ride come nightfall."

"Guard?" Jamie piped up. "You had to guard your stock?"

"Had a lot of trouble with thieves," Jason said, glancing nervously at Billy.

"Ever shoot anybody?" Jamie asked, creeping to Billy's side and touching the thin red bullet scars on his side.

"I shot a couple of 'em," Jason said, frowning. "It was my duty, them after Pa's cattle and all, but it wasn't what I thought it'd be. Made me sad."

"How about you, Billy?" Jamie whispered, touching the scars again.

"That was a long time ago," Billy said, pulling the boy around so that Jamie's elbow rested on his knee.

"The war's been over a long time now, Jamie," Heather said, rubbing the liniment into Billy's neck so that it burned deep into the stiff muscles. "We're at peace up here."

"I knew you were a soldier," Jamie said. "From the hat. But I never knew. . ."

"Knew what?" Billy asked, lifting the boy's chin away from the scars.

"Never knew anybody could be shot so many times," Jamie said, sighing. "But I've seen you use that rifle. I'll bet there were a whole lot more of them that got hit."

"Too many," Billy said sadly. "But as Heather says, that war's now over."

Jason started to speak, but Billy silenced him with a glance.

The work continued at the river. More and more sand was sifted, but except for a flake or two, it proved to be fruitless labor.

"For a week's effort, we haven't found enough gold to buy a sack of flour," Jason grumbled, kicking his pan across the narrow river.

"Be patient, son," Ben urged.

"It's hard working so long and hard for nothing, though," Jamie said, tossing the last of the sand from his pan and peeling off his shirt. "I'm tired."

Jamie splashed into the river and sat down on the bottom, allowing the current to sweep against his thin shoulders and splash water into his eyes.

"Long as you're sitting there, why don't you take yourself a regular bath," Billy said, laughing. "Your corner of the cabin's been a little riper than usual lately."

Jamie raised an eyebrow, and old Ben slapped a bit of water at the boy.

"Might not hurt if you all had a good washing," Heather called to them. "And some might remember they were given a razor at Christmas," she added, turning to Billy. "We're not all of us wild folk here."

"Not all of us," Jason said, rubbing his hairless chin.

"Soap's in the cabin," Ben said, pointing the way. "Those who aren't working can go along and bathe."

Jamie stood up, a rebellious look in his tired eyes. But old Ben slapped more water at the boy and Jamie reluctantly trudged toward the cabin.

"A good bath's likely to raise all our spirits," Heather declared. "As for me, there's little point to washing the flesh when there are no fresh clothes to put on. I'm afraid, Papa, I can best serve our company by becoming a washwoman."

Ben nodded, and the next thing Billy knew, Heather was gathering up their discarded shirts and stockings. She sent Jamie back to the cabin to fetch the bedding.

"Truly must be spring," Billy remarked as the pines beside the river sprouted shirts and blankets, stockings and underdrawers. Downstream, shielded by a large boulder, Jamie splashed away half the afternoon taking his bath. The others followed before nightfall, and Billy even bowed to the demands of his companions and shaved his beard.

"I believe a holiday's appropriate," Ben announced that night as they gathered around the dinner table. "Here we are, clean scrubbed and shaven."

"All but one," Billy said, pointing to old Ben.

"The head of a clan's bound to have his beard," Ben said, scowling. "Tomorrow we'll bring out the shears and do a bit of trimming. It's time we took a day or two off to hunt as well."

So for three days the river was left to churn its way through the rocks unmolested. Jamie was shed of his long reddish locks, and the others were trimmed as well. Billy and Jason shot two deer and a large raccoon on the far side of the river, so fresh venison steaks and biscuits topped off a fine holiday.

When morning came the next day, Ben drew them all together.

"It's time ye put yer garden in, daughter," he told Heather. "The stock needs exercise, and I'm hungry for trout. So today I'll take young Jason with me to pan the river. Heather will clear her garden, and ye two," he continued, pointing to Billy and Jamie, "will take the animals out to the meadow for fresh grass and a taste of the sun. Afterward, see if there's fish to be had from the Purgatory."

Everyone seemed pleased with his assignment save Jason.

"I know how to work stock," he protested.

"Yes, but now it's time you learned more about mining," Billy said. "I'll spell you if it becomes too irksome."

"It already has," Jason said. But he went with Ben, anyway.

Working the horses brought great relief to Billy's tired shoulders. The animals had been shut up for most of the winter in a shed no larger than a good-sized parlor in one

99

of those manor houses Billy had seen in Richmond. The mules were especially thin. It took no effort to lead them out into the open air.

Although much of the ground was still covered with snow and frozen from winter, the horses trotted with surprising ease up the hills and through the woods. The mules followed, plodding along, nibbling on a shrub occasionally. The soft grass in the far meadow proved even tastier.

"There's no need to exercise these old boys," Billy declared as he and Jamie nudged the last animal into the meadow. "They'll eat awhile, then prance to their hearts' content. If you think you can find a few trout by yourself, I believe I'll lend Heather a hand with her garden."

"I might need some help," Jamie said, gazing up with accusing eyes. Billy felt like an officer deserting his company.

"I'll be along after a while to keep you company," Billy promised. "Just let me help with the trenching."

"I suppose she's a more fetching companion," Jamie said, imitating a feminine walk.

"I suppose I ought to toss you in the river," Billy said, grabbing Jamie suddenly and lifting the boy off the ground. "But if I did, who'd I have to chase around the meadow?"

Billy relaxed his grip, and Jamie scampered off toward the river, hollering back a few jests, then shouting out a reminder that Billy had promised to join in the fishing later.

"Little brothers," Billy mumbled, recalling how he'd been one himself once. They were a nuisance; still, there was pleasure knowing he was needed.

Billy located Heather in a clearing a quarter mile past the cabin. She was busy turning the earth so it would be ready for planting.

"Can I help?" he called to her.

"Shouldn't you be with the horses?" she asked.

"They can get all the excercise and grass they need without my assistance. Jamie's busy at the river. He doesn't require any looking after, either."

"I'm not so sure of that," she said, laughing as Billy joined her.

"I promised to join him later."

"Good," she said, smiling. "There was a time when I watched over him, feeling it was my place with Mama gone. But now he's needing a man's touch, and with Papa so busy . . ."

"I know," Billy said, taking the hoe from her hands and chopping the ground. "What about you?"

"Me?"

"Who looks after you?"

"Why, I do myself, of course," she said, hitting him lightly on the arm. "Mama was wedded when she was seventeen. I require no looking after."

"No, just looking at," Billy said, smiling.

"Oh?"

"I'm afraid I'm guilty of more than my share of that."

"You've hardly any apology to make. After all, I've got little enough competition here. Surely I'm more attractive than my father or Jamie!"

"Much more," Billy said, gazing into her bright blue eyes. "You remind me of someone."

"Ellen?" she asked.

"Yes," he said, his eyes wide with surprise. "How'd you know?"

"You speak to her sometimes in your sleep. Just a whisper now and then, a sigh. You must have loved her a great deal. What became of her?"

"I went away to the war. When I came back, everything had changed."

"She didn't wait for you?"

"She waited," Billy said sadly. "I was different, though. I miss her and all the plans we made. But I had my own way to go."

Heather reached out and held his hands still. Only then did he see the deep hole he'd carved in the hard, half-frozen earth.

"If I loved someone," she said softly, "I'd follow him wherever he chose to go."

"Ellen would have come, too," Billy said, sighing. "But what kind of life would it have been, always moving around, never settling in one place, never knowing from one day to the next if I'd even be alive?"

"Not all of those scars are from the war, are they?" Heather asked, holding on to his wrist.

"No," he told her. "Your father never asked about that. But I owe you the whole truth."

"No, you don't. Whatever's been is past. In the mountains, it's not important who a person was before. It's what he is that counts."

"And what am I?"

"A good friend," Heather said, slipping her arm around his waist. "One who's been wounded by life, as Papa told us the night he brought you in. I didn't understand at first, but I do now. Billy, you're safe here."

"That's not even my real name, you know."

"Does it matter? Not to us. You belong here now. You're one of us."

Billy held her for a minute, then pulled away and resumed his digging.

"It's hard for you to admit it, isn't it?" she asked.

"Yes," he confessed, turning away.

"But I've watched you. You care."

"I've tried so many times before to make a fresh start, Heather. But each time something happens."

"Not this time."

"How can you be sure? No one paints his own future. No, it's up to life to do that. We just stumble along the best we can, hoping to get by."

"You don't really believe that!"

"You're seventeen. I'm twenty-six now. You'll learn by the time you're my age."

"You're wrong, Billy."

"Am I?"

"There's more to it all than stumbling around. What

brought you here? What made Papa go out in that blizzard? How did he come to find you, to take you in? No, there's more to it than pure chance."

"I used to believe there was," Billy said, the image of a wrinkled old Indian appearing in his mind. Beside the old man stood a boy, slight of frame, with eyes as bright and blue as Heather's. There'd been faith in that boy, a belief in the great mystery that life had been.

"I've watched you, Billy," she whispered. "Look at the way you work the soil. You've a good feeling for the earth."

"It's been so long, Heather."

"You said you're twenty-six. It can't have been that long."

"A lifetime," he said, sighing.

"No, not that long," she said, holding his hand.

For two weeks, on into late April, Billy worked the stock, helped Heather with the planting, and shared a fishing hole with Jamie in the afternoon. Sometimes he traded chores with Jason. Then, when Heather had the vegetables seeded, Billy turned his attention to hunting.

One morning as he rode his spry horse through the woods, he heard a great bellowing cry. In seconds he raced the animal back toward the river, flying through trees and around rocks the way he had across a dozen battlefields from Virginia to Tennessee.

But when he reached the river, he found old Ben Grant shoveling oceans of water at Jason McNally, both of them bare-chested and screaming like lunatics.

"What's wrong?" Billy asked, rolling off his saddle and running to where Jamie stood.

"Nothing," the boy said, holding Billy back from the river. "Look!"

Billy stared into the bottom of Jamie's tin pan. Bright flakes of yellow glittered in the sunlight.

"All this in a single scoop," Jamie said, pointing to a

glass jar near by that was filled with the stuff. "We've found it, Billy! We've struck it rich!"

"I've seen men scoop a barrelful in an hour," Billy said, shaking his head. "Then they'd spend ten years filling a thimble. No, we're far from rich."

"Not too far, though," Jamie said, his face aglow. "Wait and see."

CHAPTER 14

Billy did just that: He waited patiently for more evidence that they'd made a true strike. That evidence wasn't long in coming. The next day they sifted rock from gold, rather than the other way around. Ben traced the flow of color along the riverbed to where the Purgatory made a sharp bend a mile from the cabin.

"Ever put a sluice box together, Billy Cook?" Ben asked as they walked to the spot the following morning.

"Once," Billy said. "That what you have in mind?"

"Do ye know of a better way to work the riverbed, lad?"

"You're the expert," Billy told the old miner. "We'll need axes and a good saw if you've got one."

"I do. Jamie'll be bringing them along."

"I don't see what good we'll be till he gets here," Billy said, scratching his head. "Can't cut trees with my bare hands."

"No, but ye can pick out the best ones and clear rocks."

"All right," Billy said, nodding his head.

They'd marked two tall pines and cleared several rocks from the bank by the time Jamie arrived. Jason followed, and soon Billy and Jason were sawing through the base of the trees. Once finished, Jamie and Ben began stripping the branches and bark away. Then the bared trees were cut into lengths and set on rocks to dry.

"Seems a lot of trouble to me," Jason complained. "We were doin' all right with the pans."

"No, once you find the gold, panning's too slow," Billy told him. "You miss too much of it. The river's carrying it downstream faster than you can gather it from the bottom. With a sluice box, you shovel the bottom in and let the river do the work. I've seen a hundred yards of bottom a day cleared. Once the gold begins to peter out, you've found the rock it's coming from."

"Then what?"

"Usually you start powder-blasting. Blow a tunnel into the mountain and dig till you reach the vein. Provided there is one."

"You think there is?"

"Maybe."

"That'd be somethin', findin' a fortune way up here in the mountains," Jason said, wiping sweat from his forehead. "Who'd thought that would happen?"

"Old Ben did. All along," Billy said, sighing.

"What do you plan to do with your million, Billy?"

"I never needed a million. And I won't have it if I talk away the whole day," Billy said, splashing his friend and returning to work.

Once the sap had flowed out of the pine logs, Billy and Jason resumed their sawing, cutting planks two inches wide and five feet long from the logs. Then Ben assembled the planks into a snakelike series of two-sided boxes that were set inside one another. The whole thing was then set on legs a few feet off the ground, with a trough added to supply water from the river.

"Now comes the easy part," Ben explained, taking a shovel and throwing a pound of river bottom into the first box. The water then washed the sand down through the series of boxes, leaving the heavier pebbles and gold flakes behind.

"Throw the pebbles away, Jamie," Billy said, pointing to the sluice box. "Pick out the gold and put it in the jar, just like before."

The sluice box sped up the gathering of gold, but it was far from the easy job Ben had suggested. Shoulders, arms, and backs ached more than ever, and it was necessary to form shifts. Billy, Ben, and Jason each shoveled for two days and then spent the third fishing or tending the animals. Jamie worked the box, picking out the gold, and spelled the diggers from time to time. Heather was assigned the job of pounding the flakes and the occasional nugget into dust, weighing it, and filling small pouches with it.

"Have ye ever seen anything to match it?" Ben asked when Heather showed them the box full of deerskin pouches she'd filled.

"I'll say this," Billy said, frowning. "This is no way to store gold, leaving it out for any idle passerby to see. No, we'd best bury it somewhere."

But Ben was not fond of the idea of returning the gold to the earth.

"Better to build us a treasure chest in the cabin," Ben suggested.

"A false wall?" Billy asked.

Ben nodded. So while the work at the sluice box continued by day, each night they worked at constructing a second, inner wall onto the north end of the cabin. Inside, a crawlspace perhaps foot wide was formed. Winter clothing and the like was placed there, but its true purpose was to hide the sacks of gold dust beneath false floorboards.

"It would never stand up to a real search, but it'd fool any casual visitors," Billy observed.

"Casual visitors?" Jason asked.

"Can't ever tell when a couple of renegade cowboys might turn up," Billy said, smiling. "The next ones aren't likely to be as friendly or as handsome as us."

Heather and Jamie laughed heartily, but old Ben stomped his foot and motioned for silence.

"It may be funny to laugh at this now, but once we set

107

up that box, anybody happening by will know we're up to serious work here. Many's the bandit who's made his living off mountain miners."

Billy nodded, and the others grew solemn.

"Should we mount a guard?" Jason asked.

"It'd be a waste of too much labor just now." Ben said. "But it might not be a poor idea to carry a rifle down to the river with us."

"You don't mean to shoot anyone, though?" Heather asked.

"We have to keep the strangers out, daughter," Ben said.

"It's not our river," Heather reminded them.

"By mining law, we've got a right to our claim," Ben said, standing and then stomping his foot. "That's the way it's always been."

"You know, Ben, sooner or later people will find out," Billy said. "We'll need supplies, and the claim will have to be filed."

"I know," the old man admitted. "But the longer we have the Purgatory to ourselves, the better the chance we have of finding the real vein. I've seen it before. Some latecomer happens along and finds the mother lode. The ones who first found color end up with nothing."

Billy nodded, but he wasn't at all sure what would happen if someone did appear on the river. Now that it was almost summer, there was certain to be someone, a party of Indians or a lost teamster, some wayfaring cowboy or even other miners.

"It'll be like back on the Cimarron, won't it?" Jason asked as he and Billy shoveled sand into the sluice box. "Nobody owns the land for sure, so everyone'll fight over it."

"We'll file title before that happens," Billy explained.

"And if not? Will you fight for the gold, Billy?" Jason asked, his eyes probing for an answer.

"Not for the gold," Billy said, shaking his head. "Maybe not for anything."

"You'd stand up for Heather, though, wouldn't you? Just like you did for me in Trinidad."

"That didn't turn out too well, if you remember."

"I've seen you look at her, Billy. You'd never let her come to harm."

"And how about you, Jason McNally?"

"I wouldn't shoot women and kids, not like Pa did on the Cimarron. I could never do that. But I'd defend this place. It's my home now, and these people are my family."

"Yes," Billy agreed, returning to work. Yes, he thought, and that's how it always begins.

Pouches continued to be filled with dust on into May, but it was late spring before the first real nuggets were found. They weren't big balls of pure gold as big as a fist or anything like that. Instead they were chunks of gold mixed with quartz crystals, the biggest ones the size of a small tooth. Even so, Ben shouted and whooped like a young Comanche, and the first try was made at blasting.

"Wish I'd brought more powder," Ben grumbled as he poured powder from a small barrel into hollows he'd cut into the rocky mountainside. For fuses he used strips of old cloth. Once the fuses were lit, the miners scampered for cover some hundred yards away.

The first explosion shook the birds from the trees and caused the sluice box to collapse. The one that followed seconds later rained rocks over half the valley. Billy shoved Jason and Jamie to the ground and then covered his head with a tin pan. Ben did likewise. The worst injury was a series of stone bruises on the backs of their legs.

"Time to dig a bit," Ben announced when the smoke settled.

From that day on, Jason and Jamie were left to work the reconstructed sluice box while Ben and Billy dug into the mountain itself.

"You plan on mining the vein yourself, don't you?" Billy asked as they drove their picks into the rock, tore open the ground, and searched for the elusive quartz and the yellow streak that would make them rich.

"I always knew I'd own a mine one day," Ben said. "I

dreamed of it from the time I first dug up north in old Alec McFarlane's hole. They paid me a dollar a day and found, not much to make another man wealthy."

"Lots of worries come with ownership, Ben."

"Maybe for a young man such as yourself, Billy. But me, well, I've been honed and tempered till I feel sharp and ready for the task."

"Once you hit the vein, or think you have, you can sell out to one of those mining companies. They'll pay for the privilege of working the claim, plus give you a percentage of what they take."

"You seem to know the business awful well for a Texas cowboy," Ben said.

"I've spent time in Denver. You know, Ben, a mining town's not much of a place to raise a family."

"Raise who?" Ben asked, laughing, as he struck the ground again with his pick. "Heather's grown and Jamie's not so small. There are schools that can take a boy like that and make him into a better man than I ever could."

"You don't believe that."

"Surely I do."

"That'd be a mistake, Ben," Billy said, setting his pick aside and frowning.

"How so?" the old man asked.

"I think I know Jamie pretty well. He's like I was once, wild and eager to grow tall. He's in a hurry to be a man, and the kind of place you're talking about won't do. A boy like Jamie, he's born to the open sky, fit more for fishing the rivers and riding the wind. You can't turn him into a Boston banker. It'd choke him sure as smothering him with a pillow."

"Jamie went to school not so long ago. Frontier school, but they taught him to read and to write a decent hand."

"I can read and write, too," Billy said. "I learned at home, from my mother. But the important things, what a man needs to know to live in this country, you don't learn from books. The land teaches you. That and your father.

"It wasn't all that long ago, Ben, that my father tried to send me to school way off in New Orleans. They would have taught me useful things, like reading Greek and cheating at cards. I could have found out how to bend laws to fit my fancy. My brother went to that school, and he learned his lessons all too well. Is that what you've got in mind for Jamie, making him into a sharp-nosed Yankee businessman?"

"Lad, it's not a school that makes a man into what he is," Ben said, placing a worn hand on Billy's shoulder. "That kind of man's got a rotten core to him from the beginning. Jamie'd miss the mountain life, but ye said yourself others will come to this place. This country's running out of empty mountains, peopleless valleys. A boy ought to be around youngsters, too. Who's he to take for a wife up here, a grizzly bear or a brook trout?"

Billy sighed. The land was changing, had already changed so that he could barely recognize it. The buffalo were gone, and the Indians with them. The high country would be overrun, too. Still, he couldn't help feeling it was terribly wrong to send Jamie away to a life of four walls and a roof, a world insulated from deer and hawks, rivers and mountains.

"I'd be happy if we had two more summers in this country," Ben said, resuming his labor. "But it's not providence's way to give a man too much peace and a fortune to boot."

"Nor either one most of the time," Billy said, frowning.

"Ye'll take yer share and ride away, won't ye?" Ben asked.

"On the fastest horse I can find."

"To what, lad? Another mountain? Canada, perhaps?"

"Perhaps."

"This matter weighs heavily on me, Billy," Ben said, pausing again. "I've seen ye with Heather. If I were a king, that girl'd be the brightest jewel in my crown. She cares for ye. I see that."

"I care for her, too."

"I've seen that in yer eyes, Billy, and I know ye'd never bring her to harm. Not knowingly."

"But?"

"I'd rather ye not press yer suit with her, lad. She's not known many men, and she's little to measure ye against. I'd not like to see her promised something that wouldn't come to be."

"I'm in little position to promise anyone anything."

"Ye've been a good companion, Billy, an able worker and a good friend. To Jamie ye've been as a brother. But, lad, I can't recommend ye as a husband."

"Nor I," Billy said sadly.

"Ye understand, it's not—"

"I understand," Billy said, driving his pick into the mountain. What could I offer her? he asked himself. What kind of life could I share with anyone?

He cast it all from his mind and concentrated on the work. It was an old remedy, and it proved reliable as always. Billy emerged from the hole he and Ben dug in the mountain covered with sweat and grime, so tired he thought he'd never be able to raise his arms again. He plunged into the river, allowing its cool waters to reawaken what life remained.

Back at the cabin, Billy ate his dinner in silence, then took his leave of the others and walked out across the hillside. The stars overhead were as bright as ever, and he wondered why he felt so empty.

"Need some company?" Jamie asked from a few yards away.

Billy shrugged his shoulders and the boy joined him.

"Papa spoke to you, didn't he?" Jamie asked.

"We talked some," Billy said, sitting on a large rock. Jamie sat nearby, and together they stared into the distant darkness. A wolf howled eerily from the adjacent hills.

"Wolf?" Jamie asked, creeping over and sitting beside Billy on the rock.

"First one I've heard up here," Billy said. "Old wolves, they're going the way of the buffalo."

"Will he get after our horses?"

"Oh, a single wolf's not much threat to a horse. Old wolf, he's likely after smaller game, like maybe redheaded boys."

Jamie looked uneasy and Billy couldn't help laughing. Much of the weariness and the pain from that morning evaporated.

"Guess I should carry my rifle when I'm out here," Jamie said, huddling closer to Billy as if there were suddenly a chill to the air.

"I wouldn't let it worry you much," Billy said, patting the boy's back. "Wolf's howling . . . well, that's just nature's way of reminding men they shouldn't take too much for granted. Long ago, when only the Indians were here, men prayed before they took anything from the land. They asked the earth's permission to take a tree down, to kill a rabbit. There was a reverence for the land. Now, well, men steal everything they can."

"Steal?"

"Isn't that what you call it when you take something without asking?"

"But how can you steal from the land? Nobody owns it."

"Exactly. Nobody. We borrow from it and debts must be paid."

"I don't understand."

"Maybe it's not possible," Billy said, sighing. "Maybe it's right the old ways should die off with the buffalo."

"You could teach me."

"It's not something you can learn like letters in the alphabet, Jamie. It has to be felt in the heart."

"I feel things."

"I know," Billy said, rising. "We all do."

"But not all of us keep it hidden," Jamie said, holding on to Billy's arm.

No, Billy thought as they returned to the cabin. But like the wolf and the buffalo, he was born of the old ways. Perhaps it was too late for him as well.

CHAPTER 15

Summer arrived, bringing with it warm mornings and hot afternoons, the heat of which was broken only by a midday thundershower. Billy lost track of time as he hammered at the rock. By June a tunnel cut its way twenty-five feet into the mountainside. Jason and Jamie continued to work the sluice box, but they also cut pine logs to shore up the walls of the mine.

Old Ben continued to blast, hoping the powder would reveal the sought-after vein. But as days became weeks, Billy doubted more than ever that any fortune awaited them. The river was losing its force, and the quantity of color taken from the bottom each day declined.

"It may be too deep in the mountain to find," Billy said, leading Ben from the mine. "I've watched men tunnel halfway to China and not find the source."

"If it's there, I'll find it," Ben declared.

"How?" Billy asked. "We haven't got much powder left."

"We can get more," Ben said. "Ye can go to Pueblo. We'll have to have supplies soon, anyway."

"The moment we flash a pouch of dust, we'll have more company than you can imagine. Ben, what if it isn't there? You could spend your whole life slaving away for nothing."

"It's my life, lad."

"And what about the rest of us?" Billy asked, pointing to the river where Jason and Jamie were washing off the sweat of a hard day's work.

"Ye're free to leave," Ben said, looking away. "The passes will have thawed. Ye're due a share of the takings. I'll see ye have it."

"Ben . . ."

"Billy, I know it's not yer way to stay in one place so long as ye have with us. Ye're like those eagles up there. They come back in the summer, but come winter, they'll be off again south. I understand the urge to roam. But we've enough powder for one last blast. Ye'll stay that long, at least."

"I've never run out on a partner."

"And ye wouldn't be doing so this time. This gold's not yer dream."

"But it's yours," Billy said, sighing as he shed his shoes and shirt, then stepped into the river. "You've shared that with me, and much more. I could never just ride away."

"Then we've given ye something after all, lad."

"Only my life," Billy said, staring intently into the old man's tired eyes. "I'm not one to forget my debts."

"Debt?" Ben asked, laughing. "Lad, ye've paid that back long ago, digging here, cutting pines."

"That's not much payment for my life."

"Then there's what ye've done for Jamie, how ye've brought the life back to his step. And Heather, lad; ye've brought out the light in her eyes."

"No, it's them who've helped me."

"Aye, but I'm not certain but that ye've not been the greater giver."

Billy frowned and turned away. He doubted that. As he scrubbed the dust and dirt from his chest, he wondered what he would do if old Ben never found that vein, that long-dreamed-of fortune deep within the mountains. Could any of them stay on the Purgatory forever, slaving away on such a fruitless quest?

And deep in his heart, Billy hoped the vein wasn't there. He wanted things to remain as they were, the five of them deep in the high country, left in peace by the world beyond. Sometimes Billy prayed that his refuge would last a bit longer, another week, another month, perhaps a year. But he could never lend words to this reluctance, never voice his true feelings.

The following morning, as he laid the powder deep inside the tunnel, Ben prayed aloud.

"Lord, bring us that prosperity ye promise the righteous," the old miner cried out.

Billy wondered where such a promise was ever written. The old Methodist circuit rider who'd held meetings along the river when Billy was a boy had never spoken of rewards on earth, only of those in the afterlife.

"You think we'll hit it this time?" Jamie whispered as they hid behind a boulder.

"Your papa does," Billy said, waiting nervously for Ben to emerge from the mine. All it took was a half stumble, a second's delay, and a man would find himself blown halfway to tomorrow. Finally Ben trotted from the opening and hurried to their side. A second after the old man arrived, the ground shuddered and it seemed as if the fierce explosion blew away half the mountain. Smoke curled skyward, and what had moments before been a fine, orderly tunnel was transformed into a clutter of dislodged rock.

"It's collapsed!" Jamie yelled. "The whole thing's gone!"

Billy sighed and Ben moaned. But as the dust began to settle, something sparkled in the dim light. At first it seemed as if fireflies were buzzing about. But as the air cleared, it appeared even brighter.

"We hit it!" Ben screamed, stumbling up the hillside

past rock and splintered timbers. "It was here, after all. I knew it!"

Jamie raced after his father, and Jason came up from the sluice box. Billy moved more slowly, picking out fragments of quartz in which were embedded the heavy ribbons of yellow.

"My Lord!" Ben shouted, standing over a tear in the side of the mountain. "It's here! A glory hole! We're rich!"

Ben and Jamie linked arms and danced a musicless Highland fling. Jason jumped up and down, then dug with his hands into an immense pit of sparkling golden flakes.

"We're rich!" Jamie shouted, racing around the shattered tunnel, jumping and waving his arms about. Jason tore off his shirt and sprinkled gold dust over his shoulders. Ben stood beside the treasure and cried.

"Come and look at it, Billy!" Jamie screamed, tugging at Billy's arm. "You've never seen anything like it!"

Billy surrendered his will and allowed the boy to pull him along. Yes, there was a pit full of gold dust. Yes, beyond that the mountain revealed a rich streak of ore. There was ten years' work there, a future of wealth.

"You don't seem too happy," Jason said, leaning his gold-flaked shoulder against Billy's side. "We're all rich. We can build big houses and lie around all day, sipping whiskey or playing cards. We never have to work another day for the rest of our lives."

"Is that what you see?" Billy asked his young friend.

"Don't you?" Jason asked.

"No. I see a ton of gold, with no bank, no law for a hundred miles. It's not yours and it's not mine, not till a claim is filed, and it's dug from the rock, refined and sold." Billy sighed and stared off into the distance. "No, Jace, what I see is a dozen gunmen, a band of riders coming up here and murdering my friends. For the first time since we came up here, there's real danger."

"He's right," Ben said. "Now's the time for caution. And work."

It started almost immediately. Before, they had carried away the day's take in glass jars. Now more pines were felled to construct sturdy boxes. Into these boxes handfuls of gold dust were placed. Meanwhile, a covering of sorts was built from the rubble of the old tunnel to hide the golden scar torn into the hillside. In a week all sign of the mine was shielded, except for a stone adit, or entryway. Pine branches covered even that.

Only then was time set aside for a celebration. Ben played the pipes again, and Heather sang. An ancient bottle of scotch whiskey was produced, and pledges of prosperity were drunk.

"Never was there such a time as this, Lord," a wobbly Ben declared. "Here we stand, friends all, and rich to boot. Was there ever such good fortune?"

Billy sat to one side and sipped a small glass of the liquor. It had a heavy, somewhat smoky taste, and two glasses each of the stuff had Jason and Jamie sprawled on the floor, laughing and calling out their dreams of buying railroads and ranches, of sailing off to India or France.

"What will you do with your share, Billy?" Heather asked as he helped her clear plates from the table.

"I don't know," Billy said, fighting to keep a deep frown off his face. "I've never had much need of money. You can't buy freedom, or peace, either, with gold."

"You could go back to Ellen."

"No, she's married, I've heard, with little ones. The family ranch isn't home to me anymore. The places I loved are gone, the old Comanche camps and the burial ground high atop the cliffs. There are no more buffalo to hunt, Heather."

"There's land to be bought here in Colorado. Papa will need help managing the mine."

"If he was smart, he'd sell part interest to someone and let them manage it. I saw that ore. It's going to take a big operation to get the most out of this find; dozens of men just to dig out the ore. Then there's refining—guards, too."

"A town," she said, smiling faintly.

"Schools and churches later on. First, though, saloons and gambling houses, guns and killing."

"You know all about that, don't you?" she asked.

"All too well."

Billy opened the door and left the others to laugh and sing and dream. He climbed up the rocky boulders till he reached the crest of the mountain. Below, the Purgatory cut a frothing blue swath through the hills and peaks. He stared into the virgin forests and distant snowcapped ridges, wondering what lay beyond, wondering if there was another valley and another place there that might offer him the same warmth, the same belonging he'd found in old Ben Grant's cabin.

"What are you thinking about?" Heather asked, joining him.

"Oh, nothing, really," Ben said, turning to face her.

"I come up here myself sometimes when I'm confused," she said.

"You, confused?"

"Yes, like when you stopped looking at me. I know you're afraid of attachments, Billy, but it's too late for me. I've taken you to heart."

"You're young," Billy told her. "There will be lots of boys, fine, young, and handsome, eager to carry you off on their white steeds."

"I'm not looking for Sir Lancelot, Billy."

"Maybe you should be. All you'll find in me is a tired old Texas cowboy who tried to be more than that once. The thing is, Heather, it was enough. People are always wanting more, and when they get it, they realize it isn't what they want at all."

"Is that how it was for you?"

"When I was little, I didn't have much besides a fast horse and good friends. But the days seemed to fill themselves with life. Then the war came. I wanted to be a hero like my father. But it was the wrong war for heroes. They mostly got themselves blown apart in senseless charges or shot to pieces in ravines a thousand miles from home."

"That's all over. You've made a fresh start here. I want you to share all this with me, the gold and the happiness," Heather said.

119

"You'd be disappointed. It wouldn't be what you think. No, it's better that you forget all about me. Find someone younger, better."

"Is that what you told Ellen? I wonder if she did."

"I hope so," Billy said, glancing away and rubbing his eyes. "I'd hate to think she hurts like I do."

"Like I will?"

"No, you're seventeen. You've hardly cracked your eyes open. There are cities to see, balls to attend, a family to raise."

"You've seen cities, Billy. You came here."

"But the cities I saw changed. I was in Richmond the winter of sixty-two, when the streets were full of soldiers and fine ladies. But I also saw it in sixty-three, sixty-four, and in sixty-five, when the children were hungry and the widows sold themselves to buy bread. I rode through the shell of Atlanta, burned black by Sherman. I saw New Orleans and Nashville, their streets full of carpetbagging Yankees who filled their pockets with profits from cotton taken from scorched plantations."

"Wounds heal, Billy. People rebuild."

"I remember the first time I ever saw a town of any size, Heather. It was Houston, the first year of the war. Lord, I was so young, hardly shaving, decked out in bright blue trousers and gray coat. Papa took me to a dance a lady was having for us, the proud soldiers of the Second Texas. I met a cousin, can't even remember her name now. We danced, and she told me how brave I looked in my uniform.

"It was a fine time, Heather. There were bowls of punch as big as a kettle, with little cakes and all on the side. Ladies wore dresses of silk and lace, so delicate you'd have thought the wink of an eye would tear them. That's the kind of life you should have. With me, it'd always be slaving away over a wood-burning stove, cooking venison steaks or rabbit stew, like as not wintering in the high country or digging potatoes from your garden."

"But you'll have money, Billy."

"I've had it before—five thousand dollars once. To

spend money you have to be around people, and, well, I haven't had much luck with people, especially in towns."

"I'd go with you, wherever you want."

"Could you turn your back on your father? No. And what of Jamie? He's more than just a younger brother, you know. He looks to you like he would a mother."

"You'd never know that to listen to him," Heather said, laughing.

"Oh, you would," Billy told her, accepting her hand and squeezing it lightly. "We don't any of us weave our own lives, Heather. We do what we can."

"Yes, we do," she said. "Don't be so sure what will never be, Billy Cook. If you think Papa's determined, wait till you see me at work."

"I wish you'd trust me on this account, Heather. I know more than you."

"Oh, you know nothing about it! Sure, you've left your home behind, and left others, too, I'd wager. But you haven't stayed anywhere, have you? Well, I have. You'll have no easy time escaping me, Billy Cook!"

"I know," Billy said, releasing her hand.

CHAPTER 16

The days that followed were as long and tiring as any that had come before. As the summer heat intensified, working inside the growing tunnel reminded Billy more and more of condemned men digging their way through rock and brimstone to escape the depths of hell. Ben worked patiently, chipping away at the rocks or shoring up timbers. As for the rest of them, Billy imagined they'd be content to sell out the whole mountainside for a few thousand greenbacks.

Soon they began working in two-hour shifts. No one could stand the choking dust and confinement of the mine longer than that. Even Ben had begun to cough. In spite of wearing kerchiefs over their faces and splashing the walls with water, the dust seeped through the cloth to burn their eyes and to assault their noses and throats. At day's end Billy would discover bits of rock and dust between his toes and coating his flesh from head to toe in spite of his wearing cotton shirt, trousers, boots, and stockings.

"Look at this!" Jason complained one day as they washed the grime from each other's backs. "We're not minin' coal, are we?"

"No," Billy said, sighing. "But a mine's a mine."

"This one's eatin' us alive," Jason said, holding up his shoe and dumping out a pound of sand mixed with rock. "I sure hope I live to spend some of the dust."

Me, too, Billy thought as he listened to his friend gripe.

By the next week even Jamie and Heather were taking a turn at the mine. Billy winced each time he saw Heather's light hair smothered with dust and grime. She would walk with a stoop, and he could read the fatigue in her eyes.

"We can't dig out the whole mountain before winter, Ben," Billy finally said. "We've got the mine walls timbered, and the vein's exposed. It's time we stepped back and took a rest."

"Maybe ye're right," Ben admitted. "But I can't help myself. Every ounce we take out now's an ounce nobody can steal from us later. I worry that we'll get our claim jumped, maybe even lose it altogether to some smart Denver lawyer who can pay a government surveyor."

"You'll kill yourself, and the rest of us, too, going on like this," Billy said.

"Well, as I said, ye could be right, Billy," Ben said, wiping his forehead with the back of his hand. "We need supplies. Ye and young Jason can go. Ye'll have a bit of time under the open sky, and I can carry on with the work."

"You need a rest, too," Billy told him.

"I'll rest when I'm dead," Ben declared.

So it was settled that Billy and Jason would ride to Pueblo for supplies. A list was made, and it included cloth, ammunition, sugar, salt, flour, tins of beans and fruit, together with anything else that couldn't be raised or dug from the mountain. Powder for blasting was at the top of that list, together with a wagon to haul the supplies to the mine. Later, that same wagon could be used to transport gold back to Pueblo or north to Denver.

"Seems to me we're not leavin' you much help here," Jason said when Ben began loading eight pouches of gold into Billy's saddlebags.

"I promise I won't work any of us too hard," Ben said.

"Ye'll need two rifles in case ye come upon trouble," he added.

"Papa, that doesn't leave us much protection here," Jamie said, handing Billy a basket of food Heather had prepared. "And wouldn't outlaws be suspicious of two men riding this country alone with heavy loads in their saddle-bags?"

"What've you got in mind?" Billy asked, hooking the basket on his saddlehorn.

"I could go with Billy," Jamie volunteered. "Nobody would expect me to be carrying gold. You'd get more work done, and Jason could help guard the mine."

The idea was none too pleasing to Billy. Jason could take care of himself on the trail. Jamie would be a respon-sibility on the way to Pueblo and even more so once they arrived.

"It's all right by me," Jason said, climbing down from his saddle.

"I could go alone," Billy said.

"What if your horse threw a shoe?" Jamie asked. "What if you ran across trouble?"

"I'm used to it," Billy told them.

"I could go," Heather said.

"No," Ben announced. "It's best we do as I said, let Jason and Billy do the job."

"Papa, please let me go instead," Jamie pleaded. "I haven't seen a town in the longest time, and I'd stay clear of trouble."

"Well?" Ben asked, turning to Billy. "What do ye think?"

Billy thought less of the notion than ever, but now he was forced to stare into the long, sad face of Jamie Grant. The boy reminded Billy more than ever of himself. No, Billy thought. If my papa had kept me home from the war, everything would have been different. Ellen . . . Mama . . .

But the truth was that Billy didn't have the heart to deny the boy his right to take a man's place among them, to prove himself to a father, to a sister, to everyone that mat-tered.

"Come along," Billy said, sighing, as Jamie flew toward the horses, preparing to follow him to the passes. I have to be crazy, Billy told himself. But as they started the ninety-mile journey, he did warm to the knowledge that Jason was back on the Purgatory with Heather, able to defend not only the mine but the person who had broken through Billy's protective wall and entered his heart.

The narrow path northward through the Spanish Peaks was slow and treacherous. Peril seemed to wait at every turn. Deep snow remained in places, and rock slides blocked the natural road.

"We'll never get a wagon through here," Billy said as he led Jamie around what seemed like the hundredth dislodged boulder they'd passed that one afternoon. "We'll have to swing wide and come in from the south, along the river."

"Just as well," Jamie said. "Fewer bandits down that way."

It took three days to clear the peaks, but Billy spotted no other riders in all that time. In fact, they passed only empty, abandoned freight wagons until they reached the flood-swollen Arkansas just west of Pueblo. They'd already crossed the smaller Huerfano and Charles rivers, and fortunately neither was over its banks.

"Pueblo straddles the river," Billy explained as he turned them in an eastward direction. "Old Madill has his mercantile on the south bank of the Arkansas. We should be able to buy what we need there."

"You know a place that sells those Winchester rifles, Billy?" Jamie asked. "Like yours?"

"Madill most likely has one or two in stock."

"I'd feel better if we had some extras around, just in case there's trouble later."

"It'd be a good precaution," Billy agreed. "Best pick up a few boxes of shells, too. Anything else not on the list?"

"Rock candy'd be nice."

"Sure. We can throw it at any outlaw who appears on the river."

Jamie frowned and Billy laughed at the boy. But when

they arrived at Madill's, Billy had the old trader toss in a sack of candy just the same.

"Anything else, Mr. Fletcher?" Madill asked as he boxed the supplies.

Jamie started to say something, but Billy motioned for silence.

"We need a wagon and a good team to pull it," Billy answered, gripping Jamie's nervous shoulder and holding the boy in place.

"I'll inquire, if you'd like," Madill said. "Hank Carson's got a good draft team, and I remember George Thurman takin' a wagon in exchange for an IOU from a poker game last week."

"We'll be at the Florida House," Billy said, motioning for Jamie to follow. "All right by you if I pay you when I'm ready to leave? I have to make a visit to the bank."

"I'll be holdin' the goods, anyway, won't I?" Madill asked.

Billy nodded, and Madill agreed.

"Then we'll be by in the morning to settle accounts and view the wagon," Billy said. "Come along, Jamie."

After stepping through the door of the mercantile, Jamie grabbed Billy's arm.

"He called you . . ." the boy began.

"Fletcher?" Billy supplied. "I used that name when I rode through here last year. I've used a few."

"Like Cook?"

Billy nodded and shoveled Jamie out into the street.

"Let's find ourselves the bank," Billy said, slapping the side of the saddlebags slung over his shoulder. "I'd like to unload a little something, if you know what I mean."

"I do," Jamie said, smiling.

A few hundred yards down the street they located a place called the First Colorado Territorial Bank. It seemed far too impressive a name for a three-room picket building.

"Can we help you, sir?" asked a short man with graying hair from the far side of a small counter opposite the door.

"I'd like to talk to your manager," Billy said quietly. "In private."

"I'll see what I can arrange," the gray-haired man said. "In the meanwhile, would you mind leaving your pistol and gunbelt on the hook near the door?"

Billy glanced around him. The bank appeared to be deserted. He unfastened his gunbelt and set it on the hook. Then he motioned for Jamie to sit down. The clerk knocked once on a side door, then slipped inside a smaller room. Moments later the clerk returned.

"Mr. Talbert will be happy to see you," the gray-haired man said, motioning Billy to the door.

Billy made his way past the counter and slipped into the room. Shutting the door behind him, he nodded to a tall man dressed in a blue suit, then rested the saddlebags on the banker's desk.

"I'm Justin Talbert," the manager said, extending a sweaty hand to Billy. "I'm president of the First Colorado Territorial Bank."

"Before I begin," Billy said, lightly shaking the man's fleshy hand, "I have to know that what we discuss is kept between the two of us."

"I don't know if I can promise—"

"Then I'll have to find another bank," Billy said, grabbing the saddlebags and starting for the door.

"Hold on, mister," Talbert called. "You have to understand. I can't make promises without knowing what you're going to tell me. There are laws here, federal laws. I can't afford to violate any. . . ."

"I'm not asking you to break any laws, banker. But I have to know you can keep your thoughts to yourself. I suppose you'd say I have sensitive business to discuss. If you can meet my terms, I suspect we might do enough business in the future to make us both rich."

Billy's words had their desired impact.

"Well, sir, I believe I can give you the assurances you ask for."

"Then I guess we can do business, after all," Billy said, sitting down and gently taking each of the eight pouches of gold from the saddlebags and setting them on the banker's desk. Talbert opened the first and sprinkled the gold into his hand.

"You've made a fresh strike, Mr. . . ."

"Call me Fletcher," Billy said.

"How many of the details are you willing to share, Mr. Fletcher? Do you need financing, investors? Have you filed your claim? Perhaps a counselor . . ."

"Lawyer? No, I don't think we'll be moving that fast. No, what I had in mind was to change the dust into greenbacks. You'd get your commission, of course."

"Naturally," the banker said, smiling. "Ten percent?"

"Five," Billy said. "I'll not dicker, either."

"Then it's five," Talbert said, breaking out in a sweat. "Do all these bags hold the same quantity?"

"Why don't you fetch your scale and let's see?"

The banker nodded, then drew a small scale from a desk drawer.

"You're quite right to take precautions, Mr. Fletcher," Talbert said. "The sight of a one-ounce nugget in this country sends half the town racing for the mountains."

"Some of this I'd like to leave on deposit with you," Billy said.

"Certainly. The rest you'll need for provisions, I imagine."

Billy nodded, and the banker began emptying part of the contents of the first pouch onto the right-hand dish of the scale. He then placed a ten-ounce weight on the opposite dish. A pinch of gold, then another was added until both sides were in balance.

"I'm glad you're leaving some of this on deposit," Talbert said, taking out a white cloth pouch and emptying the first ten ounces of gold into it. "I haven't enough notes on hand. You've quite a quantity of dust here."

Billy started to tell him it was nothing compared to what was back in the mine, but he caught himself. The banker continued to weigh out the gold and record figures on paper. Billy examined each notation carefully. He didn't intend to be cheated.

"How much of this did you want in cash?" Talbert asked

when the last of the buckskin pouches had been emptied. "Two hundred, three hundred?"

"Five," Billy said, running the figures through his head. "And a bank draft for another two hundred."

"Leaving, after my commission, twenty-four hundred, sixty-four dollars, and some odd cents. I'll make you out a receipt for all this, and then we'll mark your passbook."

"I don't want the draft or the book made out in my name."

"Oh?" Talbert asked, raising an eyebrow.

"It's to be made out in the name of Ben Grant."

"I understand, Mr. Fletcher. Or Grant. We've dealt with men such as yourself at the First Territorial before. Cautious men like us will soon obtain statehood for Colorado."

Billy only smiled and watched Talbert step to his vault, turn the dial three times, and open it. The banker stored the gold, then counted out five hundred dollars in cash. He passed the bills to Billy and locked the vault. It took only another moment to write out the draft and to fill in the information on the passbook. A few stamps were affixed, and then Billy accepted the book and the draft from Talbert's hand.

"Until next time, Mr. Grant," Talbert said, opening the door.

"Fletcher," Billy said, staring hard at the man's smiling face. "See that you keep my secret, banker."

"Certainly, Mr. . . . Fletcher."

Billy stepped to the door, took his gun from the hook, and waved for Jamie to follow.

"Did you get the money?" Jamie asked as they stepped out onto the street.

"I usually accomplish what I have in mind," Billy said, nudging the boy into motion. "Hungry?"

"Well, we didn't even sample the rock candy at Madill's."

"I know a place that used to serve fried potatoes and a pretty fair steak now and again."

"As long as it isn't venison," Jamie said. "I had my fill of that last winter."

"There's a small cantina down by the river, too. If you've a taste for tamales."

"Steak and potatoes would be fine."

"I'm a little hungry for beef myself," Billy said, pointing down the dusty street to a small wooden structure.

"What about the horses?"

"We'll take them to a stable after supper. I'm starving."

"Me, too," Jamie said, following Billy toward the eatery.

CHAPTER 17

Two platters of steak and fried potatoes and half a bowl of carrots and peas were disposed of before Billy and Jamie left the café. Then they boarded the horses at a livery down the street and headed for the Florida House, a two-story hotel of the respectable type that Billy felt was appropriate for a boy of Jamie's age. It was a dollar a night for both of them, but the owner promised to throw in a hot bath.

"Sorely needed," Billy had said.

That evening they slept between clean linens, themselves scrubbed quite well by the coarse bristles of a new brush. It was the first time since Billy could remember that he'd lain on a soft mattress within clean sheets.

The following morning he had them both up with the sun. There was the wagon to purchase and the supplies to pick up at the mercantile. By noon the last detail had been attended to, and after another steak at the café, they prepared to leave Pueblo.

"Mighty short stay," declared the livery boy who brought out Billy's horse. "Most mountain folk pass at least a week here."

"I'm from Texas," Billy said.

"Sure, Mr. Fletcher," the boy said, passing the reins to Billy's hand and walking back to fetch Jamie's mount. "I'm none too smart, but I can tell when a horse's been in the high country all winter. His coat's long and his step's a little shaky."

"That right?" asked a bearded man from the door of the stable. "You just come from the mountains? North or south of the Arkansas?"

Billy turned toward the stranger.

"I don't see where it's your business one way or the other," Billy told him.

"That's not very friendly, mister," the man in the doorway said, stepping out so that Billy could see the pistol tied down on his hip. Just behind the bearded man were two other, younger men, one holding a small carbine and the other a Sharps rifle.

Billy motioned Jamie back toward the stalls, then walked slowly to the door.

"I didn't mean to be unfriendly," Billy said, keeping his hands well in front. "But I keep my own counsel, as most men who've seen their share of trouble do."

"Seen trouble, have you?" the young man with the carbine asked. "Where might that've been?"

"'Bout everywhere I've traveled," Billy said, touching the brim of his old Confederate cavalryman's hat with the fingers of his left hand. "Wasn't long ago I had to shoot two men in Trinidad. I'd rather dodge grief, but you know how it is."

The trio stepped into the street as Billy exited the livery.

"I'd choose to avoid trouble myself," the bearded man said. "I'm called Shelton, Rance Shelton. I fought with the grays myself in Missouri, then Arkansas. All I wanted to know was where you been diggin'."

"Digging?" Billy asked, shrugging his shoulders.

"Mister, half the town knows you brought in gold. Them saddlebags you had looked to carry fifty pounds of it. Nobody in weeks has put a smile on Banker Talbert's face like you did."

132

Billy frowned, then motioned for Jamie to bring the horses along.

"We could follow you," Shelton said.

"You could try," Billy said, staring hard into Shelton's eyes. "You could get yourself killed following a man into the high country."

"It's not fair," the man holding the Sharps complained. "There's enough color in these mountains for all of us."

"Then find yourself some of it and leave me the road out of town," Billy said, mounting his horse and glaring at the three would-be gunmen. "I tell you this, boys. I've shot men before for stepping out like this."

"Do tell," Shelton said, motioning his companions to one side. "So have I."

"Then you know it takes but a second for a man's eyes to close forever. Do yourselves a favor. Go find a cantina. Leave me my peace."

"Rance, he's not goin' to tell us nothin'," the young man with the carbine said.

"The boy could show us," Shelton said. "Well, boy?"

"You really do want to get yourself killed, don't you?" Billy asked, waving Jamie on down the road to Madill's mercantile. "I've given you fair warning. If I meet you on the road, someone'll be dying."

"Mighty confident, mister," Shelton said.

"I can afford to be," Billy said, spitting. "I know what I'm about."

"So do we," Shelton said.

Billy gave a final glance at the threesome, then joined Jamie. They rode side by side the short distance to the mercantile, glancing back from time to time, always finding Shelton and his friends twenty yards behind. Jamie unsaddled his horse and threw the saddle, blankets, bridle, and bit into the wagon bed. Billy had planned on riding in the wagon as well, but with Shelton around it might be wise to have one person mounted.

"You think they'll rob us?" Jamie asked as he climbed onto the wagon and released the brake.

"More likely they'll try to follow," Billy explained. "Won't be hard, not with a wagon half full of supplies."

"So what do we do?"

"Watch and wait," Billy said sadly.

"For what?"

"I'll know when the time comes," Billy told the boy. "Let's be on our way."

Under other circumstances Billy would have left the main road and headed out across the foothills of the Rockies as before. But he'd already decided to follow the Purgatory once they had the wagon, and now that they were being tracked anyway, any attention they attracted on the trail south toward Trinidad wouldn't mean much.

He'd hoped the journey back to the mountains might be peaceful for both of them. There might have been time for old stories or a song or two. As it was, they rode each day as far as the horses could hold out and made camp wherever cover offered itself. All night one or the other would keep watch.

I wish they'd just close in and have it over with, Billy thought as he made camp on the Charles River. The country seemed alive with shadows. A dozen lone riders had passed that very day, not to mention the plodding wagons of teamsters bound for Trinidad or Santa Fe. More than ever he missed the old days of the open prairies, thick with buffalo in the summer, their black hulks breaking through the yellow grassland like Moses parting the Red Sea.

Beyond the embers of his campfire, Billy saw the shadowy forms of his pursuers. It was Virginia all over again, his little command scouting or evading the enemy. It was a cat-and-mouse game, one he'd been good at. But he hadn't been dragging along a wagon and a twelve-year-old boy.

Billy wondered whether he would've stepped away from Shelton if Jason'd been along. Maybe not. Certainly not before passing that long winter in Ben's cabin. There'd been peace there for once, and it was hard to return to the old, all-too-familiar violence.

"We're leaving the road tomorrow," Billy told Jamie as

they exchanged sentry duty. "Think you can steer the wagon straight and true by yourself?"

"What are you planning, Billy?" Jamie asked.

"Yes or no?"

"Yes," the boy said, frowning. "For a time."

"Won't need to be long," Billy said, patting Jamie on the shoulder. "I'll be caught up by noon."

That next day Billy had them rolling early. He waved the wagon off the road, then rode down along the arroyo until, horse and all, he seemed to disappear. Shelton and his companions must have gotten a late start, and but for the ruts the wagon cut into the prairie, Billy might have made good their escape without incident. As it was, he was able to circle around behind Shelton and his boys.

"That's far enough!" Billy shouted, pointing a loaded Winchester at the men. "Best throw your guns down, then slide off the saddle. Left side, boys!"

"You can't do this!" Shelton objected.

"I can, and I am," Billy said, firing a warning shot that started Shelton's horse bucking.

"All right," Shelton said, tossing his pistol away. The others dropped their guns, too. Billy collected the weapons, emptied the chambers, then ordered the men down from their horses.

"What now?" Shelton asked.

"First, we bid good-bye to these horses," Billy said, slapping the horses' rears with his hat. All three animals raced down the arroyo. "Then we discard your guns," Billy explained, tossing Shelton's pistol, the carbine, and the Sharps rifle away.

"You can't leave us out here with no horses or guns," Shelton complained.

"Oh, they're here for you. You'll find 'em all in time. But I need a bit more of a start on you," Billy said, smiling. "So now I guess you'd best strip."

"What?" the men asked, their eyes wide with horror.

"Don't worry. You won't happen by anyone out here. Strip!"

The men hesitated, but when Billy swung his rifle in

their direction, each started unbuttoning shirt and trousers. Soon they'd removed their boots, stockings, vests, shirts, even their drawers. Billy collected the lot, then waved farewell. As he rode westward, he tossed one piece after another into the branches of some tree, stringing it out until each man's clothing was scattered over at least a mile.

"We'll get you for this!" Shelton's voice carried across the landscape.

Sure, you will, Billy thought as he began turning in a circle to conceal his destination. By noon he'd rejoined Jamie, as promised, and Shelton and his men were left far behind.

"I wish I could have been there to see it," Jamie said after Billy shared his experience. "How did you think of such a thing?"

"We tried it once on a Yank patrol," Billy said. "Up on the Rapidan River. Of course, back then we kept the horses, the carbines, even the clothes. They were all better'n what we had. I suppose those Yanks went back to their lines stark naked and swearing vengeance on the Confederate nation."

Twice more groups of horsemen appeared as Billy led the way to the Purgatory.

We can slip away from them this time, Billy thought as he and Jamie hitched the team long before daybreak the next day. But later, when it's known there's gold up here somewhere, there'll be others. What peace and solitude remained could only be temporary. The thought was unsettling and Billy kept it to himself.

After snaking their way up the Purgatory that final week, they finally laid eyes on Ben's little cabin. Jamie climbed down from the wagon and raced the final hundred yards to the door.

They celebrated that night by singing and dancing to Ben's bagpipe tunes. Heather baked a cake and roasted a duck Jason had shot.

"It's good to know we've got cash money," Ben said when Billy turned over what remained, together with the bank draft and the bank book.

"Someone's got to file on the land, though," Billy said. "We saw lots of riders. They'll be up here before winter."

"I don't trust those Denver lawyers," Ben said, shaking his head. "They'll cheat us for sure."

"We'll mark the property by that hog-nose piece of rock just above it," Billy said. "You can claim the acreage around the cabin as homestead. There's money to buy it if there's need. The main thing is to get there before someone else steals it from under your nose."

"I should've had ye do it when ye went for the supplies," Ben grumbled.

"We'd have been followed for sure," Billy told him. "The thing to do now is take horses, ride hard, but take care not to get followed. You can come back the hard way, through the mountains."

"It's ye that should go, lad," Ben said, resting a heavy hand on Billy's shoulder.

"No, it's you," Billy said. "Take Jason along. He knows horses, and he can shoot. If there's trouble up here, I'm the man to deal with it. You're the mining expert."

"He's right," Jason said. "He can handle a gun."

"And they'll be less likely to cheat you, Papa," Heather added. "You take the ore samples."

"It appears that I've little choice," Ben said, shrugging his shoulders. "When should we leave, late summer?"

"Immediately," Billy said without hesitation. "Serious trouble's coming, and it's better to be armed with a deed when it arrives."

"I've barely had time to speak to my son since he's come back from Pueblo," Ben complained. "Next week at least."

"Tomorrow," Billy said firmly, his tone leaving no hope of compromise. "It's important you clear the passes before anyone who might have followed our trail gets here."

"Who might have followed?" Jamie asked. "We—"

"Wagons make tracks," Billy explained. "Any fool can trail a wagon, and not everyone in this territory's a fool."

Jamie nodded, then walked to his father's side and leaned against the old man's tired shoulder. Billy led Jason off down the hillside so that the Grants could have time alone.

"Watch out for Ben, Jason," Billy said as they stared off down the river. "See he doesn't come to harm."

"You watch yourself," Jason said. "We can always run. You can't. A wisp of a boy and a girl of seventeen's not much help."

"You know I'm capable of dealing with intruders, Jace."

"I hate for it to get back to that, Billy. It's been so different up here."

"I know," Billy said, frowning. "But nothing really changes, not here, not anywhere."

"You've changed," Jason said.

But as they walked back to the cabin a little later, Billy wasn't so sure. Have I changed? Wasn't I as ready as ever to draw my pistol when Shelton stepped into that doorway?

But I didn't, Billy told himself. For once, I didn't.

An hour after daybreak, Billy helped to saddle the best of the horses for Ben and Jason. Farewells were exchanged, and provisions were packed.

"I'm not accustomed to leaving so much of my life in another man's hands," Ben said to Billy as they checked the cinches. "My Heather and little Jamie . . . Guard them as if they were made of gold."

"I will," Billy pledged.

"I know yer heart, lad. It's good to know ye're here with them. If something were to happen—"

"Nothing will," Billy said, cutting him off. "This isn't the time for such talk, Ben. Besides, it's wasted breath. You know I'd never see either of 'em in need."

"Aye, I do know," the old man said, clasping Billy's hand firmly. "Look to yourself as well, lad. We'll be home before the eagles come back."

CHAPTER 18

In the days following old Ben's departure with Jason, Billy devoted most of his time to working the diggings along the river. The vein of gold that ran along the rock wall of the mine was as rich as ever, but dislodging the yellowish rock was hard work, and the ore itself required refining.

"It's not like before," Billy told Jamie. "To get anything close to spendable gold, you need someone who really knows something about mining."

"Papa knows what to do," Jamie said.

"It's going to take equipment, too. More than just sluice boxes and such. We'd be smarter to use our time working the river for now. We'd not accomplish much inside that mine."

"Digging out the river bottom's not much of an improvement," Jamie complained. "I feel like we've searched the streambed from one end to the other. Last year Papa had us down here panning, hoping to find the vein."

"Doesn't mean there's not still color to be found," Billy said. "If you'd rather, you might dig up some of these

139

plants. Gold can catch in their roots sometimes. I once saw a ten-ounce nugget caught in the roots of a turnip."

Working outside served two purposes. Aside from the pinch or two of powder they were able to take from the river each day, Billy was able to keep watch over the valley. Each morning he felt strangely uneasy, as if someone were watching. Whenever he heard a rustling in the trees or a splash in the river, he half expected to see a band of raiders racing toward the cabin, eager to kill and to take for themselves the gold of the Purgatory.

"It seems too quiet for summer," Heather told him as they stood alone atop the mountain and watched the sunrise. "I miss Papa's pipes. I'm all the day weeding my garden with no one but sparrows for company."

"You could trade places with Jamie sometimes," Billy suggested. "He wouldn't mind giving up his shovel."

"Oh, I'm not prepared to give the crows my corn for their dinner. Jamie's a poor excuse for a farmer, always off wandering, shooting at rabbits, or fishing the river."

"You're being a little hard on him, aren't you? He's not but twelve."

"And in all those years he's never learned to stay to a task till he sees it done."

"Are you all right?" Billy asked, leading her aside. "I've never known you to be so harsh."

"I try to be fair, Billy," she said, resting her head on his shoulder. "But I can't help myself."

"Oh?"

"Don't you see? Jamie went to Pueblo with you. Now Papa's taken Jason. I'm the only one who's been up here all the while, never seeing anything save this valley."

"Nothing except your father, a kid brother, and a pair of vagabond ex-cowboys, huh? Pueblo's not much of a town. I wouldn't say you missed much."

"But Denver..."

"Isn't much of a place, either. Sure, it's beginning to build up some, but I'll bet there are more saloons than churches. I understand how you feel, though. I'd gone crazy if I'd been stranded on a mountain at seventeen with four females for company and no hint of rescue."

"Billy, would you take me down to Trinidad? For a day only? I could buy some cloth, maybe fix—"

"I can't," Billy said, frowning. "I'm not welcome there, and neither would you be if you came with me. And what of Jamie? We couldn't leave him to fend for himself. We surely couldn't abandon the river to anyone who happened by."

"I know," she said, sitting on a boulder and staring at the sunlight streaming over the eastern hills.

"You'll have your chance to see the cities, all of them," Billy assured her. "Heather, I'll bet you don't stop at St. Louis, either. Likely you'll reach Philadelphia, New York, even Boston."

"I'd need someone to show them to me. Maybe I could hire you."

"I'm not much for cities," Billy said, walking off to one side and frowning. "I told you before. I haven't found a lot of good in people. The more of them, the less good."

"You've stayed with us."

"You saved my life," Billy told her. "I owed you. You made me part of your family, so to speak. I'll look after you as best I can, but up here, not in Denver, and for certain not in New York."

"You're still planning to leave, aren't you?" Heather said, her eyes revealing a mixture of surprise and grief. "I thought maybe . . ."

"That I'd changed? I'm a little old to do that. And you're too pretty to waste your time trying to make me over into something better. You ought to spend more time talking with Jason."

"He's with Papa."

"He'll be back, Heather. Jace's a good boy, and he's fast growing into a fine man. He's only a year older than you are, and I've watched him. His eyes light up when he sees you. Give him a touch of encouragement, and you'll have yourself a proposal from him."

"I was hoping to hear from someone else."

"You said yourself I only know how to run away. What makes you think this time will be any different? It's been a long time since I was eighteen. Jason's a fitter match for you. He can take you to those cities, share your love for pretty clothes and china plates. He doesn't get itchy when he sleeps under a roof for six weeks."

"But you do?"

Billy nodded, then left her to her thoughts.

Yes, he thought as he worked the river that morning. Jason is a better choice. He's young, still a bit of a dreamer, and he's got no chest of ghosts to bury. And yet as Billy felt her eyes on his bare, sweat-streaked back as he worked, he couldn't resist imagining the two of them ten years later, sitting on a porch above the river and watching little reddish-haired children racing through it.

That dream should have died the day I rode away from Ellen, Billy thought. It was amazing that the notion had surfaced in his head at all. Even more surprising, he couldn't help wondering if Heather wasn't dreaming up something similar.

"This wouldn't be a bad place to live out your life, Billy," Jamie said as they pulled hard at the stump of a small aspen. "I don't suppose you'd reconsider and stay another winter?"

"I've made few plans," Billy said as they leaned against the stump and listened to the brittle wood splinter.

"I feel like you're a brother in a way."

"All men who love the high country are brothers," Billy told the boy. They tore the stump from the ground and then collapsed into a pile in the soft grass.

"You'd be a real brother if you took Heather for a wife."

"I couldn't do that," Billy said, brushing off dirt and getting to his feet.

"Already married to somebody?" Jamie asked.

"No," Billy said, shaking his head.

"There something wrong with me as a brother?"

"No." Billy sifted dirt from the boy's hair.

"Can't be Heather. She's always watching you, and I've

142

noticed you walking with her at night. And in the morning."

"You don't know how it is for me."

"How is it, Billy?" Jamie asked, staring up with bright eyes full of questions.

"You saw it yourself back in Pueblo with Shelton and the others. That's been my life the past ten years. Everywhere I turn, there's somebody ready to press me, to test his gun hand against mine. I've killed, and I've near been killed myself. A man like me, Jamie, he doesn't dare attach himself to folks. He can't have his mind on a wife and children when he needs to be watching some stranger's eyes."

"There's no fighting here."

"Not yet," Billy said, separating a few oddly shaped nuggets from the roots of the tree. "But it'll come. It always does."

The first hint of trouble appeared that very afternoon. Billy sniffed smoke and mounted his horse. He rode briskly up the valley until he came upon a pair of old prospectors wearing the patched buckskins that were all too common a sight in the Rockies.

"What can I do for you?" Billy asked.

"Nothin', unless you've got a nose for gold," a weathered man with white hair said. "But we'll gladly share a pot of coffee with you."

"Thanks," Billy said, sliding off his horse.

"Camped nearby, are you?" the second man, somewhat younger with dark brown hair, asked.

"Near enough," Billy said as he accepted a tin cup of steaming coffee.

"Had any luck?" the white-haired man asked.

"Not much," Billy said. "I guess most of the color must be over to the Charles River. I was through there a few weeks back. Lots of digging going on there."

"Nothing up here?" the second miner asked. "You sure? We heard someone'd made a strike up this way."

"Not gold," Billy said, eyeing them nervously. "Had

some luck with deer. Fishing's not bad. Trapping's poor now that the beaver's mostly gone."

"You trap, do you?" the younger man asked. "Don't look much like it."

"Well, I grew up working cows and horses," Billy explained. "Before the war. Then I found I liked the solitude of the mountains."

"Know that feeling," the older one said. "Still, we might try our hand at your valley up ahead."

"I said I was fond of solitude," Billy said, his voice betraying anger for the first time. "I wouldn't care for company just now."

"And if we came along, anyway?" the dark-haired man asked, reaching for a nearby rifle.

"You might wish you hadn't," Billy said, jumping to his feet and kicking the gun away. "Consider this a warning. I've got no ill feelings for anyone, but I won't have my peace disturbed. Understand?"

The two intruders nodded, and Billy walked to his horse and prepared to leave. As he rode off, he kept a wary eye on the strangers. Once he got back, he'd clean the rifles and make sure Jamie and Heather each kept one at hand. For his part, Billy'd given up going unarmed weeks before.

Two days later the morning quiet was broken by the sound of rifle shots. Billy pulled Jamie to the ground and stared down the valley in search of intruders. When none appeared, Billy realized the firing was coming from upriver.

"Look after your sister," Billy told Jamie. "See she takes to the cabin. Wait for me there."

Then Billy began threading his way through the rocks along the river, slowly creeping northward until he'd spotted the source of the gunfire. Just above the old prospectors' camp a pair of horsemen stood firing their big Sharps rifles. Bullets crashed into canvas or shattered wooden plates. Others glanced off tin pans or splintered bone.

"Can't you see my partner's dead?" the dark-haired miner cried out. "What do you want?"

Without explaining, one of the riflemen fired a shot that drove him to cover.

"Let's finish him!" one of the ambushers yelled, charging down the hillside. But the miner fixed the screaming man in the sights of an old Springfield musket and fired.

"Kelsey?" the second rifleman called as his partner's head snapped back. "Kelsey?"

"We're even now, mister!" the miner hollered. "Why don't you go back to where you came from?"

But the Sharps barked twice more, hitting the dark-haired miner first in the leg and finally in the chest. Billy saw that the ragged buckskins were torn apart and knew no one could survive such a blow.

"I got him for you, Kelsey!" the ambusher boasted. "Now we can have their gold."

Billy watched the dying Kelsey and his partner for a moment, then swung a Winchester toward them.

"Hold there!" Billy called. "Drop your rifle!"

Quick as a flash the man turned and tried to shoot. But before the Sharps could send its deadly load Billy's way, the Winchester fired.

All Billy could think, as he watched the murderer fall, was that the killing had returned, just as it always had. There was no avoiding it, no stepping aside as some had suggested. It was shoot or be shot this time, as it had been often enough before.

"Oh, Mac, I've told you not to press your luck," the dying Kelsey mumbled when Billy approached. "But you've bet your hand, and it was deuces as usual out to beat a full house."

"What'd those men do to you?" Billy asked, pointing down the slope to the miners' camp.

"We thought they might have some gold. Boys down from Pueblo said somebody made a strike hereabouts."

"Not them," Billy said, watching Kelsey's glassy eyes fade further.

"Was just like that boy to pick the wrong ones," Kelsey mumbled. Then the would-be thief collapsed.

Billy buried the four intruders together in a shallow

145

trench covered with rocks up on the mountainside. He burned the prospectors' clothes and threadbare blankets. The weapons and provisions he brought back to the cabin, together with the horses.

"You only shot one of them," Heather told him that night as they stared at the sky. "And he turned as if to fire."

"But in the end, I would have shot them all," Billy said, trembling. "If they'd come downriver."

"They've got no right to this place," she said. "It's ours."

"Is it?" Billy asked. "We've got no deed, and we've posted no signs."

"It's ours by right of first strike," Heather said firmly. "Papa has always said it's so."

"It doesn't work that way, though," Billy said sadly. "The Utes were here, and the Cheyenne and Arapaho. They owned this country only as long as they were strong enough to fight off all intruders. These hills belong to the man with the most rifles, the keenest eye. People have bled over this land, and they won't be the last."

"Will you stay?" Heather asked. "At least until Papa comes back?"

"Till then," Billy said. He was crying inside, not so much over the death of four men as for the death of a distant dream.

"And afterward?"

"That's for the stars to know, perhaps," Billy said, gazing above. "For me, well, I'm not sure."

CHAPTER 19

Billy rode often along the crests of the ridges above the river after the shootings upstream. He wasn't sure what he would do should other intruders appear. Fortunately, the few travelers he spotted appeared to be headed away from the cabin. And when a pair of riders did turn along the surging Purgatory, they proved to be no strangers.

"I don't imagine ye've done too much digging from the back of the horse, Billy," Ben said as they met beside the river.

"We've had trouble," Billy said, pointing to the charred grass that marked the miners' camp. "Four men were shot here."

"By you?" Jason asked, gripping his reins and exchanging a pained look with Billy.

"Mostly by each other," Billy told them. "The last one turned on me. I had no choice."

"We've seen lots of riders just north of here," Jason said, frowning. "Word's out in Pueblo someone's made a strike."

"That banker," Billy mumbled, slapping his knee.

"Maybe," Ben said. "But we were spied our second day out of Denver. Next morning we saw someone'd slipped into our camp, been through our goods."

Billy stared nervously at the surrounding hills.

"Are the young ones well?" Ben asked.

"Fine," Billy said, turning his horse toward the cabin. "Jamie's grown some, and Heather's pretty as ever."

"We bought some things in Denver," Jason said, pointing to the burdens on the back of two pack mules. "With the plains alive with people, it doesn't seem likely we'll get back to a town anytime soon."

"No," Billy agreed, sadly shaking his head. "You did file on the land?"

Ben pulled a deed from his saddlebag and waved it at Billy.

"I took the liberty of calling it the Old Scotsman," Ben said.

"We now own everything from the bend of the river to the cabin," Jason said proudly. "Both ridges, too. And we banked two thousand dollars in the Denver Commercial Bank."

"How did the ore prove out?" Billy asked.

"Rich enough," Ben answered. "But it will need refining, as you said. Once we finish with the river, we'll take what we've gathered into Denver, buy what equipment's needed, hire men . . . maybe even persuade the railroad to build a spur."

Billy frowned as he envisioned the raw splendor of the peaks spoiled by the railroad and the people and the towns that would follow.

"That's years away," Jason said, reading Billy's thoughts.

"Maybe," Billy mumbled, knowing time and progress had ways of eating up the minutes and hours, the months and years.

Back at the cabin, Jamie and Heather celebrated their father's return by feasting the old man with fresh carrots and potatoes dug from Heather's garden and by showing him the additional pouches of dust that had been taken from the river and the nearby ground.

Billy and Jason rode off into the trees to pass the night under an open sky.

"There're times a family ought to have a cabin to itself," Billy'd announced. Jason had come along more from obligation than desire.

"Me, I could've used a decent bed tonight," the young man said. "Pine needles may be soft, but a saddle for a pillow isn't what I'd call true comfort."

"What is?" Billy asked, shrugging his shoulders.

"A feather mattress and a warm fire. I'll say this about Pa's ranch. There was always a hot meal to be had and a warm bed."

"Miss home?" Billy asked as he spread his blankets over the pile of needles he'd gathered.

"I miss Ma especially," Jason said sadly. "Though she's gone, of course. Just now I miss old Ben's pipes and Heather's sweet voice. She's not far from marryin' age, Billy. Think I ought to ask her?"

"Talked to Ben about it yet?"

"No, but I think he'll not have any objections. I'm young, but I've got a share of the mine comin'."

"How about Heather?"

"I thought maybe you could tell me," Jason said, sprawling out on his own blankets a foot or so away from Billy. "Well, has she said anything?"

"Not that I recall," Billy said, trying to avoid Jason's eager eyes.

"But you don't think she'd turn me down, do you?"

"I gave up speaking for other people a long time ago," Billy said, closing his eyes and trying not to picture Heather in a bridal dress standing beside the river while some gypsy preacher read vows from a prayer book.

"You kind of like her yourself, don't you?" Jason asked.

"I like you, too, Jason McNally, but I don't plan to take you for a wife."

"Too ugly, huh?" Jason asked, grinning.

"And you can't cook."

149

They laughed together, then lay back and enjoyed the silence of the mountainside. There won't be many more peaceful evenings like this, Billy thought, watching a hawk soar overhead. He wondered if it wouldn't be best to leave in the morning and to set off through the mountains like that hawk, living off the land, keeping his own counsel. He worried that, as always when he took people and places to heart, pain and suffering would follow.

Billy wished just once that it would be possible to find a true refuge from the world, from the greed and violence that came with people. But the world was what it was, and he was what he'd always been, a man alone, whether camped on a mountainside, riding across a battlefield, or asleep in a cabin.

Little changed those next few days. Heather seemed to smile more, and Jamie seemed more eager to swim or to fish the river, but otherwise life along the Purgatory was no different than it had been from the moment the first flakes of gold had been snatched from the current. There were still the streambed to be scooped and the mine to be worked. The stock needed tending, and Heather needed help gathering the vegetables from her garden.

Sometimes Billy set off into the woods in search of fresh meat. And toward dusk, after eating their fill, the five of them would gather outside the cabin to watch the sun die on the western horizon, occasionally singing a sorrowful ballad or sharing each other's thoughts.

The balance of that summer should have passed peacefully. Billy wished more than anything for one more season alone with Jason and the Grants, a few last weeks before the intruding hand of humanity appeared. As it was, July was barely half over when Billy awoke to the sounds of horses splashing about in the river below the cabin.

"We've got visitors," Jason said, shaking Billy's shoulder. "Hurry and get dressed. We'll have to deal with them."

Billy sat up in bed and looked around the cabin. Ben was still snoring away in the far corner. Heather was stirring only slightly, and Jamie could sleep through a hailstorm.

"We're accustomed to this," Jason said, loading the rifles. "We've had practice, haven't we?"

"Yes," Billy said, grimly buttoning his shirt. Too much practice, he thought as he pulled on his trousers and stepped into his boots.

The two of them slowly wove their way down the mountainside. Billy spotted a single wagon perhaps fifty yards upriver from the mine entrance. Smoke from a campfire rose skyward across the river, and a small canvas shelter had been raised in the rocks.

"I think we passed this wagon on our way back from Pueblo," Jason said quietly. "A big man was driving."

"Anybody with him?" Billy asked, edging his way along the fringe of the woods. "How many guns you suppose?"

"I think there was another man. And, Billy, there was a woman."

Billy shuddered slightly. Bandits, renegades, and the like could be dealt with. Even wanderers could be persuaded to seek another direction. But a man with a wife . . . well, he came to settle, and he'd make a stand often as not.

Billy led Jason through the pines for half a mile. They were nearly on top of the wagon, and it was easy to spot a tall, broad-shouldered man sitting beside a campfire while a small, dark-haired woman stirred a kettle.

"Good morning," Billy called, stepping out from the trees.

"Mornin'," the man responded, staring nervously at the Winchester in Billy's arm.

"I'm Billy Cook," Billy said, making no offer to shake hands or exchange pleasantries. "You're on my land."

"Oh?" the man asked. "I saw no posting, no fence. Got a deed, do you?"

"From the land office in Denver," Billy said. "But even if I didn't, it'd be a wise idea to move back upriver."

"Those your diggings?" the man asked.

"They belong to me and my people," Billy said, glancing around the wagon for some sign of others. "Claim's been filed, and we're here to see it's respected."

"And just how far does this claim of yours go, mister?" the big man said, rising to his feet. "You don't own the whole river. We'll humor you a bit. I don't mind pulling back a little to keep a man happy. But I've come a long way. I mean to try my luck here. I'd guess, from the look in your eyes, there's color here."

Jason stepped out then, and the woman turned nervously toward the river.

"You got something to hide?" Billy asked. "There's more of us still. You wouldn't have somebody back there with a gun, I'd hope. It might prove a mistake."

Billy swung the lever on the rifle forward, advancing the first shell into the firing chamber.

"I've got a Sharps carbine under the wagon seat," the man said, stretching out his hands to show he was unarmed. "It's the only gun I own, so help me."

"Then who's back there?" Billy asked, swinging the barrel of the rifle toward the rocks.

"Come on out, little ones," the man said. "Ain't no one to give you alarm, mister. Just the kids."

Billy frowned as four scruffy children, three boys and a girl, emerged from the shelter. There wasn't a pair of shoes among them. The eldest, a boy of perhaps ten, held the hand of a girl of three. The other boys, sandy-haried and thin as scarecrows, looked to be six or seven.

"Oh, Lord." Jason gasped. "It's like that night back home."

"There are those in this country who'd put a bullet in you for moving in on their claim," Billy said. "I'll not have children on my conscience. Move on out by nightfall or we'll be back."

"Why bother?" the man shouted. "I told you. I'll pull back a bit, but you don't own the whole river. Look at my kids! Think they've got it in 'em to find another place 'fore winter comes? There's game here and shelter from the

152

wind. With luck we can get a cabin up, or a shanty least-ways."

"Mr. Cook," the woman said, pulling her husband back to the fire. "You'd be doin' us a favor to shoot us rather'n send us back onto that prairie. My oldest, Joshua, was shot three weeks back by outlaws. They took every ounce of our cash, all our food, even my mother's music book."

"We'll give you food and some money," Billy said.

"There's room for us all on this land!" the man shouted.

"Billy?" Jason asked. "They don't look fit to travel."

"Once you let one bunch stay, others will come," Billy said, frowning.

"We're not goin', mister," the oldest boy said then, handing his sister over to the younger boys and joining his father. "I been all my life runnin', ever since redlegs burned our farm back in Missouri. Lookee here."

Billy frowned as the boy pulled up his shirt. An ugly knife scar cut its way across the chest from breastbone to hip.

"Yank saber did that," the man said. "Killed my brother Jeff, and he wasn't fifteen years old. We weren't guerrillas, just plain farmers."

"I see by your hat you're a Southern boy, too," the woman said. "We intend you no harm. We'll keep to our own claim."

"Can't offer you much in the way of breakfast," the man said, pointing to the kettle. "Jasmine made some mush from a little corn mixed with berries. You'd be welcome to join us."

Billy shivered. He half wished there'd been an ambush, a pair of gunmen in the rocks. The woman had been bad. Children were worse. And now this story. Billy'd never been any good fighting someone he knew. Only anger moved him to act, and he felt none for the half-dozen walking skeletons in front of him.

"Billy?" Jason asked again.

"You have your breakfast," Billy told the people. "Then move on back past the bend. We'll settle the rest tomorrow."

"We'll not leave," the boy said.

"I thank you for holding your fire, Mr. Cook," the woman said as Billy turned to go. "I can see there's fair-mindedness in you."

Is there? Billy asked himself as he motioned Jason back to the trees. This settles nothing, only delays things.

"Mr. Cook!" the man called out. "I never introduced myself. As we're bound to be neighbors—"

Billy turned and glared at the man.

"I'm Price Barrett," the man went on to say. "This is my wife, Jasmine; my boys, Jody, John, and Shelby; and my daughter, Alice."

"I'm Jason McNally," Jason said, nodding to the Barretts.

"It's time to go," Billy said, waving for Jason to come along. "Don't go and get friendly. They have to leave."

By the time Billy and Jason returned to the cabin, Ben had discovered the intruders, too.

"Long before I was born, lads, there were laws to deal with claim jumpers," Ben said, loading a rifle. "If ye allow one to stay, ye can't ask another to leave. We'd best show them the road north."

"They won't go," Jason said. "They'll fight."

"Papa?" Heather asked, her eyes full of dread.

"There are little kids with them," Jason said. "I watched my pa shoot a dozen farmers one night. Then his men gathered the women and the little ones, even those that couldn't walk, into a circle. They shot them down like mad dogs. I won't do that, not here, not ever!"

"Ye won't fight to hold what's yours?" Ben asked. "Well, Billy?"

Billy turned away, ignoring the unspoken question.

"Ye know what'll happen, lad?" Ben said. "The whole valley'll be full of them, half-starved renegades who'll steal everything we've worked for. Some'll dig, but others'll do their best to lie and steal and cheat us out of what we take from the mine."

"I know," Billy said, nodding. "But I'll make no war on

children. Maybe if we offer them food, some money, they'll—"

"If we give them leave to go, ye know they'll tell others," Ben said sadly. "It's hard, doing what needs to be done, but—"

"You can't shoot down innocent women and children, Papa," Heather objected. "It's what the English and the Campbells did after Culloden. I remember your stories."

"That was different," Ben said, staring angrily up the valley.

"It was a killing of innocents," Heather said. "How was it different? You mean because there are only a few this time? You mean because we're only doing it so we can be richer?"

"I won't let you shoot them," Jason said, stepping forward until he was eye to eye with Ben. "I should've stood up to my pa back on the Cimarron, but . . . I don't know. Maybe I was too young, or too small, or too scared. I'm not anymore."

"You can't keep them out forever, Ben," Billy said. "Someone was bound to come along. You can always sell the mine. We've got enough gold already to make ourselves a good living. It's not worth the taking of more lives."

"What is, lad?" Ben asked. "Would ye not fight for yer home, for yer people?"

"I would, and I have," Billy said. "But this fight would only be for gold, and I've never found it could buy me what I most need. I'm sorry, Ben, but if they choose to stay, you must let them."

CHAPTER 20

The Barretts moved half a mile upstream, but they refused to go farther. Ben offered money and supplies, issued warnings, and made threats, all to no avail. In a week the foundation of a cabin took shape, and each morning Barrett and his children would wade into the river and pan for gold.

Billy made frequent trips to the makeshift shelter Mrs. Barrett and young Jody had fashioned from pine limbs and canvas. Mostly he brought game to feed the half-starved children. From time to time he would offer advice on building the cabin or give the little ones a chase through the shallows.

"Never should've let you talk us into comin' upriver," Barrett grumbled as he picked a flake or two from the bottom of his pan. "Half the gold in Colorado's likely back down there."

"No, the river's pretty well played out all along," Billy said. "But I suspect you can take a few hundred dollars out before the river freezes."

"It's not fair," Barrett said, over and over. "Poor folk never have a chance."

"We'll do all right, Pa," Jody said, working all the harder.

"You could take our offer and head back to the plains," Billy said. "I can probably get you three hundred dollars."

"We're stayin'," Barrett said defiantly. "It may kill us, but we'll work this claim through till there's no sand in the river."

Mrs. Barrett would shake her head sadly and find a fresh cup of coffee for Billy and sometimes a biscuit or crust of cornbread.

"He's had hard luck of late," she'd say, dropping her head. "You'll forgive his manners, Mr. Cook. We're grateful for the meat."

Billy nodded and went on his way. In truth he enjoyed his visits with the family, but Barrett's grumbling bothered him. The man's eyes held that flicker of greed that was all too often found in gold camps.

Things got no better as others arrived, sometimes singly, more often in clusters. Most were wayfarers, ex-soldiers who hadn't been able to return to the settled life of a farmer. A few families appeared, stopping over on what had become a nomadic exodus from the old Confederacy. Very few knew anything about mining. Most expected nuggets the size of a man's fist to fall from the sky.

"I don't mind the people," Ben said to Billy as they stared at the smattering of cabins and shelters. "It's what they bring with them."

Where only weeks before the Purgatory had flowed swift and pure, it now had grown dark and muddy from the panning. Suds from washing and all manner of refuse flooded the stream. The laughter of the Barrett boys had given way to the profane boasting of thieves and loafers. Soon the quiet of the night was pierced by screams and gunshots. People died over a poker hand or a stolen pouch of gold dust.

"You knew it would happen, didn't you?" Jason asked

Billy as they watched a pair of miners shove a man named Matt Hooper down toward the river. Hooper'd stuck his knife through the ribs of a drifter, all on account of a silver-plated watch.

"You all know the penalty for stealin'," Price Barrett, who'd become the unelected mayor of the camp, cried out. "A man's property is sacred, and old Hooper here killed as well. We've got no jail. It's got to be hangin' or nothin'."

"Don't hang me, boys," Hooper pleaded, dropping to his knees. "I was halfway drunk when I did it."

"Hang him!" screamed a pair of miners from the back of what had grown into a restless mob. "Hang him!"

Hooper pounded the ground and sobbed terribly as Barrett motioned to a man holding a large rope. The rope was thrown over a branch and a noose was fashioned around Hooper's neck. Hooper was then hauled up into the air, screaming and coughing out his life. It was neither an easy nor pleasant way to die.

"I wish we'd left this place," Jason said, turning away from the scene and staring into Billy's hardened eyes. "It's as bad as Pa's ranch."

"It's people," Billy mumbled.

"No, people are usually better'n this," Jason objected. "Like the Grants. They took us in."

"You already forget Hart Stephens?"

"It's just the gold, Billy. I felt like that myself when we took the first of it out of the river. I wanted to make sure I got my share even if nobody else got a pinch. It's the dream, I guess. All of a sudden I saw myself rich."

"Maybe," Billy said, gazing below at Price Barrett. There stood a man with a good wife, children, all Billy'd once hoped for. But where another man might hunt or fish for the food his family ate, Barrett would pay one of the others two days' dust for a bag of flour and a couple of trout. Other times he'd send Jody up to the cabin to find Billy.

"We've got nothing to eat, Mr. Cook," the boy would say sadly. And Billy would mount his horse and lift the boy up beside him. Together they'd ride down the valley and track down a deer or shoot some rabbits.

"You work the hides, Jody, and you can make moccasins for yourself and your brothers and sister," Billy said when they returned.

"I'll pay you back one of these days," Jody said, as always. And as the boys returned reluctantly upriver, Billy couldn't help thinking, Barrett's going to ruin that boy.

By August's close, a ramshackle town of sorts had sprung up, beginning at the edge of Barrett's diggings and spreading itself along the west bank of the river a hundred yards. Purgatory Rocks, the people had named the place. A federal marshal had arrived to impose law and order, after a fashion, and a land office had opened to certify claims.

The marshal's arrival did little to stop the gambling, but it did cut down on shootings. Soon a small bank and a general mercantile appeared, both owned by a Kansan, Trace Atwood. The only other buildings were a small hotel and a large brothel. Billy was less than pleased to discover that most of the gold passed from the miners' pockets into the mercantile's cash drawer or into the broad pockets of Rance Shelton, who watched over the ladies at the brothel.

"I figured we'd run across each other again," Shelton told Billy the first day they saw each other in town. "By an' by, we may have business."

As for Atwood, the clever banker loaned money against a man's claim, then took the property when the payments weren't made on time. Since most of the loans went to pay Atwood's high prices for flour and dried beef, the Kansan couldn't very well lose.

"I've seen it all before, up in the Bighorn country," Billy told the others back at the cabin. "Flour's thirty dollars a sack. A potato takes a full day's panning. Soon that Atwood'll own the whole river."

"Without lifting a pan or a shovel once," Jason said angrily.

Atwood wasn't content to buy up just the modest diggings of the drifters, though. As autumn painted the aspens orange and scarlet, he rode to Ben's cabin and called out a greeting.

"I'm prepared right now to buy you out, Mr. Grant," Atwood said. "Lock, stock, and barrel."

"But I'm not prepared to sell," Ben said. "I know my business. I don't plan to give away a lifetime's work."

"I'll offer you a fair price," Atwood protested. "Ten thousand dollars plus a percentage of our take for the next ten years. After costs, that is."

Billy smiled and shook his head. The mine had yielded close to that much already. And if he read Atwood right there would be more costs than profits.

"I don't believe my partners woud favor such a sale," Ben said, eyeing the others.

"Might want to consider it a while," Atwood said. "Soon word'll be out that you've got a real strike here. Men whose diggings aren't doing well will hang around yours. Outlaws may raid your camp."

"We can take care of ourselves," Billy said, glaring at Atwood. "I wouldn't want to be the one to be behind any such raid, either."

Atwood left reluctantly but returned at least once each week to make a fresh offer.

"Maybe we ought to sell out, Papa," Jamie said after a pair of drifters had fired twice at the cabin. "This is no good place to be now."

"I'll never sell my dream to that banker," Ben declared.

"Atwood was right about one thing, though," Billy said. "We need more help to work the mine. And we need guards."

"It'll cost," Ben pointed out.

"Sure, but you'll increase the profits," Billy said. "There are men about who'll work for their keep plus a little dust."

"Winter's not far away," Heather said. "Soon it will be cold, and the worst of those men will leave."

Billy knew that was true, but he wasn't sure they'd be willing to leave empty-handed. Sometimes men facing winter with neither food for their bellies nor gold in their pockets were driven to desperate acts.

Ben sifted through the clutter of lean-tos and tents of the placer miners, picking out ten who seemed to know what they were about. None minded hard work, and all were glad to abandon the meager takings along the river for the promise of steady work, wages, and plenty to eat.

In no time the newcomers split the central shaft into two parallel tunnels. Nuggets were carved from rock, and ore was made ready for processing. Billy and Jason cut trees and sawed planks for a large cabin beside the mine. Ben supervised the work while Jamie and Heather gathered food and attended to the cooking.

As the wind's bite grew harsher, most of the miners upriver abandoned their diggings and headed east. The girls at the brothel soon followed, and except for the gamblers who frequented Price Barrett's cabin, most of the drifters left for greener pastures.

The river's about played out, Billy thought, watching a group of would-be millionaires riding out along it. Most of these men won't be back. The lucky ones have a few pouches of dust to show for their efforts.

Finally, the federal marshal left, too, selling his small cabin to Atwood for three times its worth. The land office closed, and Billy half expected the banker to go, too.

"There won't be much protection around here now the marshal's gone," Atwood told them on his weekly visit. "I'll raise my offer. Twenty thousand."

Ben laughed, but Billy frowned. They were sending two wagonloads of ore down the river to Trinidad. The gold in that ore alone would fetch half of Atwood's price. Six men would go along, so there would be fewer guards here than ever.

"You're crazy to live up here like rock snakes when the whole of Denver could be yours," Atwood told them. "Pure Rocky Mountain crazy."

"We've grown used to the mountains," Billy said. "Maybe you're the one who ought to head out. There's not much gold being taken out of your holdings. Tell you what. I'll buy you out . . . for fifty dollars."

"What?" Atwood said, color rushing into his face. "Those claims are worth a hundred times that, a thousand."

"Got any better offers?" Billy asked, laughing. "That's the kind of offer you've made Ben. This mine's going to produce a lot of gold in its time."

Ben laughed again, but Billy watched Atwood's fiery eyes. If it were possible to read another man's thoughts by gazing at his face, Billy thought he surely knew the banker's mind.

You'll never see the profits from that mine, Atwood seemed to be saying. And you haven't heard the last from me!

Even as the banker rode away from the cabin, Billy sensed a new, strangely ominous feeling in the air.

"Mark my words!" Atwood shouted up to them. "You will sell!"

CHAPTER 21

Two days after Atwood's visit, Billy was going about his business as usual, teaming up with Jason and Jamie to place the roof beams atop the walls of the new cabin. Ben had gone to Trinidad with the ore wagon, and the hired men who remained were needed in the mine.

Two hours after dawn Billy heard something stir in the nearby woods. Memories of the ambush above Trinidad flashed through his mind. Atwood's words seemed to echo through the crisp autumn air.

"You will sell!"

Billy fingered the handle of the pistol on his hip and slowly turned around. But instead of a dark-eyed gunman, Billy discovered young Jody Barrett. The boy stood as if frozen, his eyes revealing only a trace of their former warmth.

"I'm kind of busy, Jody," Billy said, hammering a wooden peg into place. "We've got about an hour of work to get done this morning."

"Can I talk to you, Mr. Cook?" Jody asked.

"We can hunt a little later."

"It's not about that," Jody said, nervously shifting his feet.

"Go on," Jamie said, taking the hammer from Billy's hand. "We can do this."

Jason nodded his agreement, and Billy turned the roof over to his companions. Jody led the way deeper into the woods, then sat down on a boulder.

"We'll go see if we can scare up a buck or two," Billy said, resting a hand on the boy's shoulder. "Your ma can salt the meat, put some of it away for winter."

"Mr. Cook, my pa doesn't know I'm here."

"He doesn't usually, does he?" Billy asked. "I've seen it before. Gold fever. A man loses his senses."

"Mr. Cook, you've got to listen to me," Jody said, grabbing Billy's arm and holding it tightly. "This man was at our cabin. Mr. Atwood hired him."

"What man?" Billy asked, sitting beside Jody on the rock.

"I never saw him before. He was a stranger, but I could tell he was the kind that shoots people. The man who shot my brother had eyes like his, all cold and scary."

"Are you saying Atwood hired him to shoot someone?"

"You," Jody said, trembling. "That's why I came. You've been good to us, to Ma especially. She sent me. If they find out . . ."

"They won't."

"There was another man with him," Jody went on to say. "I knew him. His name's Rance Shelton."

"Should've known," Billy said, sighing. "Maybe you ought to stay up at old Ben's cabin for a time. Jamie'd welcome the company."

"If they find out I'm gone, they'll know I'm here," Jody said, shivering. "I have to go back."

Billy nodded and stood up.

"You watch yourself," Billy told the boy. "Thanks."

Jody nodded sadly, leaned against Billy's side for a moment, then raced off through the woods. Billy returned to the river, keeping a wary eye out for trouble.

"Jason, go bring the men from the mine," Billy said

when he rejoined his friends. "Jamie, run up to the cabin and wait there with Heather. We're likely to have trouble this morning."

Jamie looked up in surprise, but Jason's quick response silenced any possible questions. As Jamie trotted off toward the river crossing, Billy picked up his rifle and cast his eyes down the valley.

"What is it?" Jason asked, reappearing a short time later with the four men from the mine.

"Maybe nothing," Billy said, pointing upriver. "But we may have visitors shortly, and I think we ought to be prepared."

"Visitors?" Jason asked.

"It appears our friend Atwood has hired someone to pay us a visit or two," Billy explained. "This is the perfect time. Half our people are on the way to Trinidad, and we've got a year's work to finish before winter hits."

"So, what do we do?" Jason asked.

"You men work on these roof beams," Billy said, pointing to the heavy beams nearby. "Jason, you and I will stand watch."

"We can defend ourselves, Billy," Jack Olson said, pointing to Billy's Winchester.

"We're not at war just yet," Billy said. "If you hear shooting, though, send someone up to the cabin for rifles and ammunition. Get to shelter. I don't want to get you all shot up."

"We wouldn't be any too happy about that, either," Jack said, smiling nervously.

"Let's go, Jace," Billy said then, motioning for Jason to follow.

The two old friends started up the river, keeping an eye open for strangers. Halfway to the Barretts' cabin, a horseman appeared.

"Billy," Jason said, nervously cocking his rifle.

"I see him," Billy said, feeling his insides grow cold and hard.

"Guess you weren't expectin' to see me again, were you, boys?" the rider called out.

Billy stared hard into the taunting face of Hart Stephens. No, Billy thought, but bad luck has a way of reappearing.

"Your partners are both dead," Jason cried out. "I guess it's your turn."

"Tall talk for a bar stool," Stephens said, laughing.

"Did you come to say something or just to get yourself shot?" Billy asked. "Well?"

"I heard the old Scot is gone just now," Stephens said. "Mr. Atwood said he thought you might be a better man to do business with."

"It's not my mine," Billy said, shrugging his shoulders.

"That's not how I see it," Stephens said. "You put your name on a paper. I'll worry about the old man."

"You'd best worry about me," Billy told him. "I don't forget when a man puts bullets in me."

"I don't forget things myself," Stephens said, riding closer. "Those were friends of mine you shot in Trinidad."

"Friends?" Billy asked, laughing. "You never had a friend in your life unless maybe it was a bottle of whiskey or a twenty-dollar gold piece. You rode on out of town without blinking an eye. Don't tell me you had any second thoughts about that."

"You had the fire in your eyes then, Cook. Now you've been digging in the ground most of a year. You've gone soft. The craft's gone from your hand, I'd say."

"Ready to find out?" Billy asked, raising the barrel of the Winchester.

"Oh, we will before this is over. Count that as a promise. But just now I'm a messenger making you an offer. If you decline it, you'll hear more from me."

"That might not be healthy," Billy said, firing a warning shot into the river beside Stephens's horse. The animal reared high in the air, and it was all the gunman could do to keep his saddle.

"We will be seeing each other," Stephens said when the horse settled down.

"I'll be here," Billy called as Stephens turned his horse and prepared to ride away. Just then Billy spotted a flash to his left.

"Get down!" he yelled, pushing Jason to the ground.

Seconds later a shot rang out, kicking up a spiral of sand a foot from Billy's head. Stephens waved his arms about, and two more shots followed. Billy crawled into the trees, followed closely by Jason.

"I should've known," Billy grumbled, searching the opposite hillside for signs of the bushwhackers. "Once I saw Stephens, I should've known Shelton would be nearby."

"I'm worried about Ben," Jason said, huddling behind a rock. "Could be they had men waiting for him."

"I sent our best two shots along with the wagon," Billy said, firing at a shadow on the ridge across the river. "There are seven of them, and they've got good open ground around them. What's more, Atwood would have had to send someone downriver, right past us. I've had my eyes open for anyone going that way. Atwood's no common thief. He wants the deed, not just the gold. And especially not ore that needs processing."

"And what about us?" Jason asked.

"Oh, he wants us dead. There's no doubt about that."

"Sure is a shame to disappoint a man so often," Jason said, smiling as he took aim at the far ridge.

Three figures emerged from the trees a hundred yards away, firing their rifles and trying to make their way toward Billy's rocky refuge. Jason fired at the smallish man on the right; Billy calmly, carefully took aim and hit the one in the center first, then sent the third rolling down the hillside.

"We make a pretty fair team, don't we?" Jason asked, nodding with satisfaction at the death of the three gunmen. But before the smoke even cleared, fresh gunfire erupted.

"There," Jason said, pointing to the powder smoke curling up from the rocks beside the Barrett cabin.

Billy frowned as he led the way through the trees toward the new enemy. Clearly three more rifles were firing. The shots shattered tree branches overhead, but the rate of fire was slow, careful.

"Heavy caliber," Billy declared. "Not repeaters, though."

"Price Barrett's got a Sharps," Jason pointed out.

"Be careful of your aim," Billy said. "There's a window just past the rocks."

"I saw that boy this morning, Billy. You did seem pretty much prepared for Stephens."

"Yes," Billy said sadly. "And I suspect the boy must have known his pa was involved."

"And still he came," Jason said, shaking his head. "Boy like that deserves a better father."

Well, he's likely to be rid of the old one, Billy thought as the firing continued.

After ten minutes, a pair of horsemen appeared. Billy recognized them as friends of Rance Shelton. Neither had much experience, though. They charged through the river right at Billy's position, but the Winchester's rapid firing turned them away.

"We'd have held the Yanks at Sharpsburg if we'd had a thousand of these guns," Billy said. "I'm going up the ridge. Keep an eye on them, Jace. Once I'm atop them, it'll be short work to finish this business."

Jason nodded, and Billy slipped away into the trees.

It was not difficult for Billy to make his way through the tall pines to a place overlooking Price Barrett's cabin. Soon he had circled around behind the place so that he could see a pair of riflemen crouching in the boulders.

The large man on the left was clearly Barrett himself. The other was Rance Shelton. Stephens was on the far side of the cabin.

"It'd be a real fine idea if you boys were to freeze like icicles in winter!" Billy cried out, watching them all closely.

Shelton leaped over the rocks, only to be hit by Jason from downriver. Stephens took advantage of the distraction to race to his horse and climb onto the saddle. Billy turned to shoot, but Barrett fired, splintering the pine beside Billy's cheek. Instinctively Billy turned and fired, then stared in horror as the back door of the cabin opened and young Jody Barrett appeared at the moment his father's head snapped back from the impact of Billy's shot.

"Price!" Mrs. Barrett cried out, rushing past her son to her dying husband. "Oh, my God!"

Billy glanced once at the fleeing Stephens, then stepped slowly toward the cabin. Jody walked to his father's bleeding corpse, touched his mother's shoulder, then turned to face Billy.

"I killed him," the boy mumbled.

"No, I did," Billy said, shuddering as he realized all that had transpired.

"He was my pa, and I killed him," Jody said, sinking to his knees as the other children crept out of the cabin and gathered around their mother.

"I . . . tried . . . I tried to give him a chance to . . ." Billy began.

"I saw," Jody said. "He wasn't a bad man, you know. It was the fever, like you said."

"Yes," Billy agreed, drawing the spindly boy to him with a wave of the hand. Jody's shivering shoulders nestled themselves into Billy's side, and Billy could feel the tears dribble down his arm.

"He was an able farmer," Mrs. Barrett said bitterly, rising to her feet. "It was the war, I suppose. Then there was Joshua."

Billy nodded, then reached down and lifted Jody's thin frame up so that the boy's tear-streaked face rested on his shoulder. The boy muffled a cry and then spoke.

"I couldn't let him do it, not after . . ."

"I appreciate it, Jody," Billy said, shaking as the boy sobbed. "I'll see to it you and your family are provided for."

"There's no need," Mrs. Barrett said, gathering the little ones to her. "It wouldn't be right. Jody didn't go to you hoping for any reward."

"I know that," Billy said as the boy gripped him tightly. "But I feel a responsibility here."

"You have none," the woman said, drying her eyes. "It's for me to tend my family now."

"I understand," Billy said, prying Jody's fingers loose and setting the boy on the ground. "I'm very sorry things turned out this way. Price Barrett was a lucky man, having a good wife and fine children. To risk all that was folly."

Mrs. Barrett tried to smile, but it wasn't possible.

"I'll be by to look in on you in a day or so," Billy said, lightly touching the other children on their heads, then turning back toward the river. Jason was waiting and watching, his eyes equally sad.

"Wasn't anything else you could do, Billy," Jason said as they walked slowly back toward the mine.

"I could've left last spring," Billy said, kicking a stone into the river. "I knew this would happen. It always does!"

"Billy?" Jason said, touching Billy's trembling arm.

"Send someone down to bury the dead ones, will you?" Billy asked. "I've got to get away from here for a while."

Jason nodded, and Billy handed over the Winchester. Then he disappeared into the pines.

CHAPTER 22

Billy sat alone atop the mountain for half the afternoon, watching a pair of eagles circle overhead. It took him back to an earlier, better time when the world was simpler, less fraught with anguish and regret.

It's come back, he told himself as he finally started back toward the cabin. I must have been dreaming to think I could escape.

Even worse, he knew it was not over, not so long as Atwood had gold, and Hart Stephens had bullets.

For a few weeks an uneasy peace settled over the Purgatory valley. Atwood kept to himself, leaving the bank only to eat and to sleep. The dead, save Price Barrett, were laid to rest in the little graveyard behind the abandoned brothel. Barrett was buried on a small rise above his cabin. Billy helped Jody carve a pine marker, and Heather found a few wildflowers for the grave.

By the time Ben returned, the workers' cabin was finished, and Billy had crafted beds of pine for the men. Heather filled mattresses with pine needles, and even

Jamie pitched in, carving a weathervane for the roof and purchasing a table from the hotel.

"You've made progress," Ben said after examining the cabin. "But Jamie says there's been trouble."

"Atwood," Billy said, sighing. "We killed most of the ones he sent, but there'll be others."

"I spoke to someone in Trinidad about the ore," Ben said. "A mining company will be sending a man to examine the vein. They're eager to lease us equipment to do the refining here. Or maybe to form a partnership."

"Sell out," Billy said, frowning. "It's not worth it."

"To Atwood? Not after what he's done, lad."

"To the mining company. Retain a percentage, Ben. You've got money in the bank now. It's a poor time to die."

"I've never been run off my own land, Billy, and I don't plan to start now."

"There are others to consider," Billy said, pointing toward Jamie's strawberry-blond head as the boy raced along the river.

"And what about you, lad? Will you stay?"

"I wish I could say no," Billy told the old man. "But that's the trouble with me, Ben. I don't let myself be run off, either. I always stick."

Atwood made one final effort to buy the mine, offering a full thirty thousand for three-quarters interest.

"You've nerve even coming up here!" Billy yelled at the Kansas banker. "Next time I'll shoot you dead."

It wasn't long afterward that Hart Stephens reappeared. Sometimes a rifle would bark in the middle of the night. One of the miners was wounded carrying ore from the mine. An attempt was made to burn the workers' cabin.

"It's all come to a head," Billy said, loading his Winchester one morning. "I can feel it. If not today, surely it will happen before the end of the week. Atwood's got to move on us before winter. He can't wait six or seven months, with the whole valley frozen and no way through the passes till spring. His men have no winter quarters. That hotel's got gaps in the planking a buffalo could run through."

172

So Billy took Jason into the pines above the mine, carefully studying the valley beyond, making sure no one edged his way past them. Then, an hour before noon, shots broke the stillness.

"There," Jason said, pointing to powder flashes on the far ridge. The shots were aimed at three men loading ore into the wagon.

"Let's go," Billy said, snaking his way through the trees toward where the miners huddled behind the wagon. Suddenly more shots were fired, only these came from behind them.

"Ambushed," Billy said, diving to the ground. "That Stephens! You can say this much for him. He knows his business."

Jason managed to crawl behind a rock wall and fire, allowing Billy to reach the shelter, too.

"We're in for a time of it, Billy," Jason remarked as the rocks shattered with half a dozen shots.

Billy kept his head down and tried to determine the source of the firing. But rocks and trees blocked his view.

"We'd better get clear of this place," Billy said. "It's worse than being in that canyon back on the Cimarron."

"We near got ourselves killed that time," Jason said, firing at a shadow on the ridge above. Billy fired, too, so rapidly that powder smoke spread over the rocks.

"Ready?" Billy asked. Jason nodded, and the two of them fired twice more, then raced for the cover of the pines. Their shots were answered, and Jason cried out in pain.

"I'm hit, Billy!" the young man called out, crawling between two pines as Billy rushed past. "I'm hit!"

Billy turned abruptly and headed back to his friend. Jason's leg was bent strangely, and blood had already begun to seep through his trousers.

"Well, I guess I didn't run fast enough this time," Jason said, firing his Winchester as Billy tore the young man's pants leg apart and made a temporary binding for the wound.

"Doesn't look too bad," Billy said, sprawling on the ground beside his friend.

"Yet," Jason said. "Next shot, though, may do a little better job of it."

Billy frowned. He felt on strangely familiar ground. How many times had he crouched in the woods, waiting for a charge, knowing any minute the final bullet might find its way into his heart? No anger, no sudden fury surged through him. He was cool, poised.

"Hold your fire," he whispered to Jason.

"Billy?" the young man asked with alarm.

"Let them think they've finished us."

Jason nodded, then fired a final shot. Billy passed the next few moments refilling the Winchester's magazine, and Jason did likewise.

"I think we got 'em!" a voice called out from the high ground above.

"Make sure," ordered a second voice, one Billy recognized as belonging to Hart Stephens.

Billy and Jason lay perfectly still and listened to the sound of heavy footsteps on the ground nearby. Soon a ragged drifter stumbled out of the pines in front of them.

"Over here!" the drifter yelled. "I see 'em."

"Take aim," Billy whispered. "Now."

Billy searched the ridge above for some sign of Stephens while Jason raised his rifle and fired, knocking the drifter backward down the mountain.

"So, they haven't finished you yet, Cook!" Stephens yelled. "Glad you didn't disappoint me."

Billy bit his lip and patted Jason's shoulder.

"I know," Jason said. "You've got to try to get in behind him. I'll be all right."

Billy wanted to say something, but he could find no words for his feelings. Instead he slipped back through the pines and began to make his way uphill in order to get a better shot at Stephens. Billy hadn't moved ten yards, though, when he came face-to-face with Jamie Grant.

"Good Lord, Jamie," Billy said, pulling the boy to the ground. "What are you doing up here?"

"I heard the shooting."

"So you ran up here without so much as an ounce of sense in that brain of yours! You might've brought a rifle."

"I did," the boy said. "Two. I left them with Jack Olson down at the wagon."

"That was wondrous smart, crawling into an ambush."

"I couldn't just let them get killed," Jamie said, pulling away from Billy's outstretched hand. "It's what you would have done."

"Probably," Billy said grimly. "But I thought you were smart."

"Maybe I've been in your company too much."

"Maybe," Billy said, smiling faintly. "Take my rifle. I've got the Colt."

Jamie took the long rifle, then followed Billy closely up the ridge. To their right, Jason continued to duel with Stephens. Below, Olson and his companions were fending off others.

"We should have ridden over to that bank and killed Atwood," Jamie whispered. "Two of those men near shot Papa. Jim Morgan and Henry Turner are dead."

Stephens had planned it well, Billy thought, straining to climb the steep mountainside. Coming at them from all sides. But now they were fighting Billy's kind of battle, weaving through wilderness, striking from nowhere and then vanishing again.

Once they reached the crest of the ridge, Billy located a perfect vantage point overlooking the whole of the valley. The sole problem was that it was already occupied by a sandy-haired marksman dressed in buckskins.

"Wait," Billy said quietly, motioning Jamie to one side.

The boy hid behind a tree as Billy crept forward. The gunman's attention was on the battle taking place below, and Billy was able to get behind him. Billy took a deep breath, drew his pistol, and charged forward. Before the outlaw knew what had happened, Billy had knocked him

175

senseless. He bound the unconscious man's hands and feet, then waved Jamie over. When the boy arrived, Billy placed him carefully behind three large rocks. "Watch the ridge, Jamie," Billy warned. "Keep an eye on this one, too. If anybody down there moves, shoot."

"I'll try," Jamie promised. "I haven't done a lot of shooting, Billy. What if—"

"You'll do fine," Billy said, touching the boy's forehead as he had once touched a brother with the same name. "Watch yourself, too."

As Billy wove his way down the ridge, he tried to locate Stephens. The one above was out of the fight, but Billy was unable to detect any sign of the leader. Across the river, a pair of riflemen were having a rough time against Olson's Winchesters.

So this is it, Billy thought as he made his way down the hillside. He wished he still had the Winchester. Or that the gunman atop the ridge had carried something better than an ancient Springfield. But the old Colt had served well in the past.

As Billy crept onward, he finally spotted a figure to his left. The man was closing in on Jason.

"To your left, Jace!" Billy screamed, then fired rapidly at the shadowy form.

Jason's Winchester fired and the man dropped to the ground, groaning and clutching his knee.

"Stephens!" the wounded man yelled. "You still there, Hart?"

They all got an answer when Stephens suddenly stood up and fired three times with a revolver. The first shot went harmlessly through the pines. The second glanced off a boulder and tore through Billy's left hand. The third shot brought a cry of pain from the top of the ridge.

"Billy!" Jamie screamed.

Billy had no time to answer. Stephens fired both pistols, filling the air with bullets. Billy managed to roll behind a pine tree and rip the sleeve from his shirt. He then bound the broken flesh of his hand and reloaded the Colt.

"So, is it just you and me now, Cook?" Stephens yelled. "I've been waitin' a while for this!"

Billy listened for sounds of gunfire. Jason's rifle had grown silent, and only muffled moans came from Jamie.

"I'm ready, Stephens, whenever you are," Billy answered. "How do you want it: front, back, or sideways?"

"A man's just as dead whichever," Stephens said, racing off to one side and firing into the woods. Billy saw but a flash of his enemy, but Stephens was clearly close by.

"You all right, Jamie?" Billy called. But there was no answer, not even a moan this time, so Billy tried to work his way back to the boy. But Stephens had other ideas. Suddenly the gunman appeared a few feet away.

"It's over," Billy said, firing quickly. Stephens slumped against a tree, and Billy watched as a circle of red grew until it spread across the man's midsection.

"Nothing's over," Stephens said, staggering forward and raising his pistol. A mixture of fear and terrible hatred filled the killer's eyes, and Billy stepped back. Before he was able to bring his pistol level, a shot split the air and Stephens fell sideways.

"He's finished this time," Jason said, dragging his leg as he crept forward.

"Watch the wounded one," Billy said. "I'm going to check on Jamie."

"Jamie?" Jason asked, wrinkles etching themselves into his forehead. "Oh, God."

Billy winced as pain flashed through his hand. But it didn't stop him from racing up the hill. Down below, the riflemen across the river raised their hands in surrender, and Jack Olson collected their guns.

When Billy reached the crest of the ridge, he discovered Jamie lying in a pool of blood beside the Winchester. A deep hole had been shot in the boy's hip, and Billy did his best to plug it with the remnant of his shirt. He then lifted Jamie onto one shoulder and started down the hill.

"There's one up there that needs picking up, too," Billy said, pointing to the mountaintop.

"We'll attend to that," Jack said, helping Jason down the hill.

Billy then continued with his limp burden toward the cabin, ignoring the shattered bodies he passed along the way. It was just another in a long line of battlefields, and Jamie was only one more battered friend that had shared a violent life.

CHAPTER 23

Billy managed to reach Ben's cabin with his precious bundle before collapsing. He knew nothing for several hours. When he woke, he found his left hand swollen and quite purple. Pain throbbed its way through his whole being. Jason's leg was shattered by the bullet, and Jamie lay on a bed in the corner, white as newfallen snow, with breathing so shallow it seemed at any moment death might steal the little one's soul.

"You're not supposed to get yourself shot," Jason said, smiling from his bed. "Look at us—I'm laid up with a busted leg, and you've got a hand half blown off."

"And Jamie?" Billy asked.

"Lost a lot of blood," Jason said, sadly glancing at the boy. "He should've stayed out of it."

"It was his home," Billy said, frowning. "He had as much right to be there as anyone."

"They hanged Atwood," Jason said, pointing out the window. "From the roof of his bank. Ben says there wasn't but a thousand dollars left in the vault. And he was goin' to buy us out!"

Billy rolled off his bed and stumbled over to Jamie's side. The boy seemed somehow smaller, younger than before. Reddish blond hair fell over his forehead, and Billy brushed a few strands from Jamie's eyes.

"I'd have had it different," Billy whispered.

He felt his heart harden as it always did at such times. Caring exacted a heavy price, and a wise man kept his feelings to himself.

Heather and Ben entered the cabin then. Heather made her way to Billy's side while her father continued on to where Jamie lay.

"It's not your fault, you know," she said. "It's the way he's always been, eager to grow up faster than he should."

"I could've stayed with him on the ridge, protected him."

"No, you couldn't," Ben said, looking over. "Ye did what ye had to."

"I could've followed Stephens into town, shot him then," Billy declared. "I should've tended to Atwood. I knew what was bound to happen."

"You're not a killer," Heather said.

"I'm not?" Billy asked, his eyes suddenly wild. "I've shot people. I've let others I—I care about get hurt, maybe killed."

"You did what you could," Heather said, kissing his forehead. "We would never have survived if not for you and Jason."

But still Billy wondered.

In the days that followed, Billy never strayed far from the cabin. Sometimes he would catch Heather washing Jamie's face, softly singing one of her lovely ballads.

"You're too rich to die, Jamie Grant," she'd tell him. "A good Scot never gives up!"

But as the boy's face grew thinner, and he failed to regain consciousness, Billy worried more than ever. The chill autumn wind whined through the valley, and Billy bundled himself in his coat and walked out on the mountainside.

Gazing up at the stars, Billy recalled how close they'd used to seem. Once, when he'd stood atop the cliffs overlooking the Brazos back home in Texas, he'd felt the wind tear open his shirt and reach deep inside his heart. Then the stars had been just beyond the touch of his fourteen-year-old hand. In the other half of his life that had followed that moment, he had never again known such perfect peace.

"I've not been a religious kind of a man." Billy spoke to the distant stars then, swallowing a tear. "I've not been the kind of man I wanted to be, nor walked the road I set out on. Mostly I've killed and been killed in turn, so to speak. Everyone and everything I've cared about—loved—has been stolen away, Lord. I don't know why you've spared me all this time. But if I could swap places with that little one inside, I would. Since I can't, help him to come back to the people that love him. He never hurt much of anybody, and I expect he'll do a lot of good if he has the chance."

Billy walked back and forth beneath the stars for half the night, shivering from the cold, yet lingering.

"What on earth are you doing?" Heather finally asked, joining him in the wee hours of the morning.

"Praying," Billy said, softly touching her hand.

"You could pray inside where it's warm," she said, pulling him toward the cabin.

"No," he said as they walked. "I don't know any other way. I'm not much of a head bower. I've got to look God in the eye, so to speak. Be out there where He is."

Heather smiled at him, then gripped his hand tightly.

"Jamie's awake," she whispered. "Pale and hurting, but alive. Jason's feeding him some soup."

Billy stopped for a second to stare overhead, then quickened his pace toward the cabin. When they entered, Billy discovered she was right. Little Jamie sat up in his bed, silently sipping soup from the spoon Jason pressed to his lips.

"Glad you came back," Billy said, touching the boy's cold, thin fingers. "We've missed you."

Each day afterward Jamie grew slightly stronger. It sad-

181

dened Billy to see the pain in the boy's face, but life had returned, and that was enough to be thankful for. Pain could be endured.

Billy passed those hard days of late autumn hunting deer, often alone, with Jason on crutches and Jamie in bed. Sometimes, though, young Jody Barrett would happen by, and the two of them would set off together.

"Winter's about here," Heather declared finally. "Some of the men are heading back to Pueblo tomorrow."

"Winter's hard in the high country," Billy said.

"I hear the Barretts are staying, though. The rest have left."

"But Ben will stay," Billy said, sighing.

"We couldn't leave now, not with Jamie just getting his strength back."

"There are doctors in Pueblo to help."

"The wound's healing nicely, and fresh air will do more for mending spirits than a town would."

"Winter's a hard time to spend alone," Billy said sadly.

"You're not alone," she said. "You've got us, the Barretts, and Jason McNally."

"I can't stay here, Heather. When I set off into the peaks, I thought maybe I could find a place missed by everyone else. But that's not possible. I must've been crazy to think I could find peace here or anywhere."

"We need you, Billy."

"No, you don't."

"I do."

"For what?" Billy asked, staring into her shining eyes. "I'm too old and too tired to bring you what you'll want from life. Get to know Jason. He's dependable as the day's long, and younger, too. He'll give you his heart completely, not just for a time and not because the girl he once loved is beyond his touch. You can build a life with a man like Jace."

"And you?"

"I'll find my way. Don't worry about that."

"I will," she said, sadly clasping his hands.

Billy tried to leave without any long good-byes, but

they were unavoidable. He spoke quietly with Jamie, remembering their hunting trips and the long hours spent digging gold from the riverbed.

"I'd have you keep something for me," Billy said finally, passing into the boy's small hands the old Colt revolver that had seen four years of war and an even tougher seven afterward.

"You ought to keep this for your son," Jamie objected.

"No, you're as close to one of those as I'm likely to happen across," Billy said, coughing. "I'd like to think it's in the hands of somebody who cares. Jason can teach you how to load and clean it."

"Why don't you stay?" Jamie asked. Tears crept into the corners of his eyes, and it was difficult for Billy to rise.

"Some men are just bound to roam, I suppose," Billy said, touching the boy's shoulder a final time before turning away.

"I'll see your shares in the mine are protected," Ben said. "We've got quite a lot of cash now. How much would you like to take with you?"

"Three hundred ought to see me through the cold months," Billy said.

"That's hardly right," Ben complained. "A thousand, at least."

"Half that would be more than I could take without it bringing me trouble," Billy said, smiling. "I'll write you if I get settled somewhere."

Jason accompanied him outside, leaning heavily on his crutch and fighting back emotion.

"We'll miss you some, Billy," Jason said finally.

"I'll be disappointed in you then," Billy said. "You ought to be serenading Heather, whispering fine words in her ear, making plans for all the little ones you'll have running around this place."

"You've been more than just a friend," Jason said, gripping Billy's hand tightly. "More like a brother."

"I know," Billy said, fighting to shake loose of the sadness.

"Don't forget you've got a home here. You know, Billy, there are only so many roads a man can take to nowhere."

"I know, Jace."

But as he headed out down the Purgatory, he wondered how true it was. Roads had taken him to a hundred places, past a thousand nowheres. Yes, he thought grimly as he rode. Roads had taken him to many places, but they'd never brought him back to any of them.

He nudged the horse into a slow gallop and gazed a final time back at the river. Yes, here he was again, riding on into the dark unknown, swallowed by the black cloud of loneliness. It would be a cold, cruel winter, and he wondered if spring would ever again promise such brightness as he'd found that one year in the Spanish Peaks.

ABOUT THE AUTHOR

G. Clifton Wisler comes by his interest in the West naturally. Born in Oklahoma and raised in Texas, he discovered early on a fascination for the history of the region. His first novel, MY BROTHER, THE WIND, received a nomination for the American Book Award in 1980. Among the many others that have followed are THUNDER ON THE TENNESSEE, winner of the Western Writers of America's Spur Award for Best Western Juvenile Novel of 1983; WINTER OF THE WOLF, a Spur finalist in 1982; and Delamer Westerns STARR'S SHOWDOWN, THE TRIDENT BRAND, and PURGATORY. After twelve years teaching in the Texas public schools, Wisler now devotes his time to writing and speaking to school groups. He lives in Garland, Texas, where he is active in the Boy Scouts.